N GRAY

Deadly Pattern

BOOKS

By N Gray

The Dana Mulder Suspense Thriller Series

Deadly Pattern

Devil Mountain

Chasing Evil

Nightcrawler

Through determination and will,
we can do anything we set our minds on.
Here's to a better 2021.
- N Gray -

Vinci Books

vinci-books.com

Published by Vinci Books Ltd in 2025

1

A CIP catalogue record for this book is available from the British Library.

Paperback ISBN: 9781036701758

Chapter One

BIANCA STRETCHED HER LEGS. That familiar click in her right knee sent a jolt of pain up her leg; the movement caused her to move her upper body, and pain from her shoulder made her wince. She relaxed one muscle at a time, and, after a few seconds, the pain dissipated. Having another scar once she'd healed wasn't comforting, but it was just another scar to add to the one that went down her right leg.

When Bianca had first arrived at the hospital, she had shared a room with another patient before being wheeled into surgery. Now she had a private room and wondered whether her insurance had approved it in full, because she didn't have money to pay the difference should there be an outstanding balance.

Her room was clean with the standard eggshell-colored walls, starched bedding, and repulsive hospital smell—disinfectant mixed with body odor and the lingering stench of a corpse or two.

Her shoulder throbbed, and the joint felt tight. She tried

to move it, but it was strapped tightly in a sling against her body. It was an old sports injury that had worsened when she had fallen. She couldn't remember how she had fallen on the sidewalk; she was walking one second, the next thing she had woken in the back of someone's truck. The kind man had offered to take her to the hospital. The next day, she was scheduled for a rotator cuff repair.

Gently massaging against the bandage on her shoulder, she felt something, and wondered whether the orthopedic surgeon had done an arthroscopy as he had promised or if he had gone full on butcher on her arm. She shuddered at the thought.

Footsteps sounded; a light knock on the door was followed by a nurse beaming at Bianca as she entered. "Morning, my name is Mary, and I'll tend to you today. How ya feeling?" The nurse wore a tight white bun on top of her head, had clear crystal-blue eyes, and a warm smile to match her happy demeanor. She carried a blood pressure monitor and reached for Bianca's arm. Her powdery perfume wafted in behind her, causing Bianca to stifle a sneeze.

"Okay, I guess. When will I see the doctor?" Bianca sat up, using her uninjured arm. Her right arm throbbed in the sling as she moved even though she kept it still. She leaned against the pillow, breathless. She could stay where she was. She didn't have the strength to sit all the way upright; that position was as good as it would get.

"He's busy with other patients, but you'll see him soon," Mary said while leaning Bianca forward, fluffed her pillows then helped her lay back again. "You comfy now?"

Bianca nodded. "And my dad, is he here yet?"

"No, but I'll send him in the moment he gets here." Mary squeezed her knee through the starched bedding.

"Don't fret. I'm sure he'll visit you soon." She cocked her head with a sympathetic smile. "You hungry?"

"Not really. Maybe thirsty." Bianca felt blood drain from her face. The sudden movements didn't agree with her, and bile rose, which she swallowed, tasting the bitter aftereffects of the anesthesia.

Mary smiled knowingly. "It's just the morphine. It makes patients a little nauseated soon after the procedure. Don't panic with what I'm about to do." Mary lifted the bleached covers. "I'm just going to remove the catheter."

Bianca felt a gentle tug on her lower body but didn't notice the little tube leaving her. She did have an over-whelming need to urinate though.

Mary unhooked the bag from the side of her bed and placed it on the trolley that stood against the far wall.

Bianca relaxed, hoping the feeling would disappear, but it didn't, and she needed to go. "Okay, I need the bathroom now." Bianca slowly sat upright.

Mary smiled, pulled the covers all the way back and helped her off the bed.

Bianca wobbled slightly, but Mary steadied and guided her to the small bathroom in the corner.

Once Bianca was done and back in bed, Mary left the room but returned after a few seconds, wheeling a trolley full of food and a glass of juice to Bianca's bedside. She set the plate of food onto the over-bed table with cutlery and a plastic cup with three capsules. "Eat." She sat in the chair beside the bed and watched intently.

"Are you going to watch me eat the whole time?" Bianca lifted the lid to see scrambled eggs and toast.

"They say eggs and dry toast go down easier on the first day. Don't mind me. I'm here to ensure you're okay and can eat something before you take your pain meds."

She jerked her chin at the plastic cup holding the capsules.

Bianca ate slowly and sipped even slower on the orange juice then paused until the nausea passed before she continued eating.

Mary watched Bianca the entire time. Frosted-colored eyes gleamed at her once she finished. "Now for your medicine, it'll help with the pain. I promise." Mary pushed the plastic cup closer along with the half-full glass of orange juice.

Bianca swallowed one capsule at a time, finishing the orange juice.

Mary removed the plate and glass and handed her the remote for the television against the wall opposite her bed.

She flicked through the channels—all six of them—eventually stopping on a cartoon about a mouse. Bianca's eyelids felt heavy. Her skin tingled, and her body relaxed one muscle at a time. The medication took its hold on her.

When Mary closed the door behind her, Bianca's eyes fluttered open, alarmed when she heard the door shut with a distinct sound of a lock turning.

Bianca's heart hammered against her chest. Why was she locked in?

Chapter Two

I WATCHED the black whirlpool in my favorite mug as I stirred my coffee. The warm liquid tasted like coffee for once and not burnt tar. That's only because I was the first one at the office and had started the pot. I was usually the last to arrive, but I was up early this morning.

"Where did these come from?" I asked Marc, pointing at the bouquet on my desk.

"Dunno. They were outside the door when I arrived. The card had your name on it, so I placed it on your desk while you were in the kitchen making coffee. Do you have a boyfriend we don't know about?"

"No! No time for that." I surveyed the card. It only contained my name printed—not even the company who had delivered the flowers. I shrugged. "They're pretty. It's a shame I have to throw them away."

Marc arched an eyebrow.

"Don't give me that look." I chuckled.

Marc arched the other eyebrow; it was his party trick.

"I don't trust flowers from unknown senders." I walked

toward the kitchen with the bouquet and placed them near the trashcan for discarding.

When I reentered the office, Marc was tapping a wooden stirrer on his desk while yapping away on the phone to some poor schmuck who probably said something he shouldn't have. I grinned when red blotches climbed his neck and spread to his cheeks. Yep, someone was pissing him off.

Marc was my boss. He had opened his private investigative business about five years ago. Our workload consisted mostly of couples who suspected their partner of cheating and wanted proof for the lawyers. We also investigated cold cases of missing people, theft, and surveillance. Every now and then, we worked with the police on active cases—but not often.

Before Marc was a PI, he had been a detective, and before that a marine. He still stayed in shape but lately had developed a soft belly and only shaved once a week. I'd met him when I was hospitalized; his wife Rachael was my roommate. She had been in a car accident, and he had lived in the ward with her while she had been in a coma. He had told me about his business, and I had told him about me, and he had offered me this job. Unfortunately, his wife, who was also his receptionist, didn't survive. They had discharged me the same day as her passing. I had attended her funeral a day later to offer my support. And since Rachael's death, Marc hadn't hired another receptionist. Her desk stayed empty but clean, and we all answered our own desk phones. And, as they say, the rest was history.

The doorbell chimed, the door slammed shut, then an old-ish white male entered, knocking over one of the visitor chairs. He made a beeline for me and didn't stop until he was at my desk.

I rose from my seat, hand extended.

His hands were sun-kissed with age spots.

"I'm Dana. Can I help you?"

The man shook my hand, nodding profusely, and swallowed hard. It sounded like it hurt. His eyes were red-rimmed, forehead beading with sweat, and his clothing clung to him like a second skin.

I glanced outside to see the clouds in front of the sun and the wind blowing; it wasn't that hot. Whatever was happening with this man was serious.

"Do you have any water?" the man asked, his tongue sticking to the inside of his mouth, and he swallowed again. "Sorry. Where's my manners? I'm Ned."

"Yeah, sure." I grabbed a polystyrene cup from the holder, filled it with chilled filtered water and handed it to him. "Please, sit." I motioned for the visitor chair near my desk.

He gulped the water with a satisfactory *aah* sound.

I filled it again and handed him the full cup. "You don't have an appointment." I was expecting a phone call any moment, so whatever the guy wanted, he had to be quick.

"No." He swallowed, blinking misty eyes. "No appointment, but you come highly recommended—the best in Illinois actually."

Smart move, we loved flattery.

"What's the matter, Ned? You seem"—I waved my hands in his general direction— "disturbed by something."

He emptied the cup, placed it on my desk and wiped his eyes with the palms of his hands.

Marc ended his call, and I knew he was listening without having to look in his direction.

"My daughter is missing."

I raised an eyebrow. "Have you tried the cops, Ned?"

They were the first line of contact in missing children cases. They had the resources to find kids quicker. We didn't, unless they were cold cases, and there was no rush to solve those.

"You don't understand. I dropped her off at the hospital yesterday morning for a procedure on her shoulder. But, when I returned to fetch her, she wasn't there. When I spoke to the administrator at admissions, she said my daughter was never there."

"I understand how stressed you must be. But again, I must ask, did you go to the cops? They're better equipped to handle missing children cases. We don't get involved in active cases."

"She's an adult." His voice was clipped, concise. "And yes, I was there. Filled in that damn form and was told to come back in a couple of days. By then, she could be dead. And besides, they're all busy with that accident on the highway anyway."

Oh yes, I had been watching the highlights this morning when carnage on the highway flashed in red on my TV screen—forty-eight cars, two trucks, and a school bus. They needed all available resources.

"But they have detectives who work missing cases," I confirmed again.

Ned sighed, glanced at Marc then back at me. "She didn't run away from home, and she doesn't have a boyfriend. She really isn't that kind of kid. Yesterday, the detectives said they'll see what they can do and contact me. When they didn't, I phoned today, and they said the hospital staff didn't even have her on record. They also spoke with the doctor, and he denied ever consulting with her. It's like she disappeared, and nobody saw anything. I'm back to square one. The police think she has a boyfriend I wasn't aware of and left town with him." Ned leaned back in the visitor's chair, looking deflated and miserable. "We're close. Especially after her mother died. She wouldn't leave me like that without saying where she was going."

I glanced in Marc's direction, arching an eyebrow. This was the usual spiel we got from parents with so-called missing children. How many moms and dads really knew their kids and what they were up to?

Marc shrugged and nodded. Fine. We would hear Ned out and see how we could help. I would also see which detectives were working his daughter's case.

"Okay, Ned, give me all the details." I switched on my phone and tapped the voice recording app in the top right corner without having to look. "You don't mind if I record you?"

He nodded.

"Great. I want to know everything, from the moment you woke up yesterday until you walked through our door." I grabbed the nearest pen and pulled my notepad closer. "Sorry if I sound unsympathetic, but can you afford our rates?" I gestured toward the sign on the wall near my desk.

Ned checked the posted per-hour cost and nodded with widened eyes. "I own a construction company. It's fine."

We were not cheap, but we got results, and we got them quickly.

"I can take this case, Dana," Marc offered.

"It's fine, Marc. I got it."

"You have enough on your plate."

We'd had this conversation before, and I wasn't about to get into it with him again, especially not in front of a client.

"I. Got. It. Marc."

My desk phone rang. It was my other client. I glanced at Marc and asked with my eyes.

"Let me get that for you," Marc offered, punched numbers on his phone and answered my call.

I returned my attention to Ned.

He reviewed every single detail he could remember. He gave me all the names of the doctors his daughter had seen, along with the reasons, and when.

Chapter Three

BIANCA WOKE FEELING groggy and nauseated . The last thing she remembered after eating the eggs was drinking the capsules. Then she slept.

Lifting the covers, she realized she was wearing different clothing. Someone had changed her underwear and nightie while she had slept. She lifted her arm to her nose and noticed her skin smelled of coconut. While she slept, they had cleaned her and covered her in the body cream. They had touched her. She whimpered and pulled the covers tighter around her body.

Unsure of the time or day, since she didn't have her cell, she was unsure how long she had been asleep for. The room had no windows or clocks, and the television had no time. She was hungry, therefore must've slept at least eight hours.

Bianca's shoulder ached. She hadn't recognized any of the capsules and vowed to never drink them again, even if the pain in her shoulder killed her. She knew and under-stood shoulder pain, but the unknown was scarier.

The door lock sounded, and Mary entered, wheeling a

trolley. Bianca sat and leered at her. Her shoulder throbbed with a constant pain no matter how she rested her injured arm.

Mary parked the trolley, lifted a plate and stood in front of Bianca; her smile reached her eyes, crow's feet prominent. She proffered the plate of food.

"Hello, sleepyhead. For dinner, you have rump steak, roast vegetables, fries, and a cheese sauce on the side."

"How long was I asleep?"

"A while."

"Did you change my clothing?" Bianca twisted the covers against her chest.

"Yes, but don't worry, I didn't look." Mary winked.

Bianca shuddered at the thought of lying unconscious while Mary touched her.

Mary removed the silver cloche, assaulting Bianca's nose with heavenly aromas, and her stomach rumbled. Mary pulled the over-bed table closer and placed the food on top and neatly lay the cutlery beside the plate. Next to the plate was a tiny plastic cup with the familiar three tablets.

Bianca eyed them suspiciously then glanced up at Mary. "Has my dad come yet?"

"No, dear, not yet. Are you sure you told him you were at this hospital?"

"He dropped me off." Her voice raised, sounding angry, but she didn't care. "And where is my phone? I need to call my dad."

"I'll look for your belongings. But I think they misplaced them during your operation."

"How convenient!" Bianca crossed her arms, not believing a word. "When will I see the doctor? Surely, I don't have to stay here for more than one day for such a minor procedure!" Heat crept up her face with unchecked anger, and her body felt hot.

Mary leered at her. "Do as you're told, Bianca. I said he will come when he's ready."

Bianca flinched as if she were hit.

They stared at one another for a heartbeat, then Mary's icy-blue eyes defrosted. Her demonic smile returned to that friendly yet dangerous crescent shape and placed her hands on her hips. "Eat up," she said sweetly. "And I'll see what I can do about the doctor coming by. Okay?" Mary was as chipper as ever. The sound of her voice was grating.

Bianca bit her bottom lip to stop venomous words from flying out of her mouth. She was thinking of a couple of swear words or where Mary could put her food but decided against it. She didn't know Mary or what she was capable of doing and had gone to great lengths to abduct her. Bianca was also in pain and couldn't defend herself.

Mary skipped out of the room. Once again, the familiar click as Mary locked the door.

Bianca eyed the tablets. She ate the food, one delicious bite at a time, and felt guilty for enjoying it, knowing full well something was off with nurse Mary. She realized she couldn't confront Mary due to her fluctuating mood whenever she didn't approve of Bianca's behavior. Until she knew more about her situation and why she was here, she wouldn't anger Mary. But she wouldn't drink the tablets again.

After she ate, she grabbed the plastic cup holding the tablets and climbed off the bed. Standing over the toilet bowl, she poured the three capsules inside and flushed, watching them swirl around and disappear.

Bianca pressed her ear against the door; all she heard was the thrumming hum of the air conditioner. And then she heard … footsteps. Her heart sank to her feet, and she bolted for her bed. With the sudden movement, she pulled her right arm skew, which sent bolts of lightning up her neck and pain down her arm. The door clicked open. Bianca lay still, her eyes shut tight. Footsteps heavier than Mary's edged in, coming closer. Gripping the pillow with one hand, the other the mattress, Bianca knew how to lay still—to play dead. It was fight, flight, or just lay there and pretend you're asleep. Someone brushed her hair out of her face. Beads of sweat peppered her forehead. Surely, they would know she was only pretending.

"What did you give her?" The whispering voice was a baritone.

"The usual three," Mary replied full of confidence.

"Did you see her swallow them?" His voice held a warning Bianca recognized and trembled.

A hand slapping flesh echoed in the room, followed by a soft whimper. They scuffled, then their footsteps were quick as they exited, followed by the door slamming and locking shut with sounds of crying in the hallway.

Bianca sat upright, shivering in disgust. That was too close. She pulled her knees to her chest and hugged her legs, rocking herself to sleep.

Chapter Four

THE WAITER BROUGHT another glass of ice-cold water. My late-lunch/early-dinner date was late, again. Sipping on the cool liquid, I glanced up when the restaurant door opened. The sun was shining into my eyes, momentarily blinding me and bathing the person in a silhouette of darkness. All I saw was a shadowy figure standing in the doorframe. The figure approached. Placing my glass on the table, I kept my eyes on him. I could only see who it was when he sat across from me.

"You're late." I narrowed my eyes at him.

He grinned back at me. "You know I'm always late. You should've just ordered, keep your mouth busy while you wait for me."

I replied by punching him in the arm.

He faked being hurt, almost falling off his chair. The people around our table stared at us; when Donnie growled, they were very busy with the dish in front of them.

I rolled my eyes and stifled a laugh. "You're such a clown."

"Well, we're blood, so that makes you half a clown."

I couldn't argue with my brother no matter how dimwitted he acted for his age; he was my family, and I loved him.

"I can't stay though. Sorry, I know this is our monthly late lunch, but I'm working a case." He arched an eyebrow alerting me to the fact it was an important case that could either make or break his career. He was ambitious, and so far, he always got what he went after.

"I need your help," I said with my bottom lip sticking out like I used to do as a child when I wanted something to go my way.

He shook his head. "You know I can't, Dana." He sighed.

"The father was at your precinct yesterday. His daughter is missing from a hospital where she was supposed to have had a shoulder procedure done. And the detectives haven't taken him seriously. She may be an adult, but she hasn't left town, and, from what her father says, she doesn't have a boyfriend. The detectives called the hospital, and the doctor denies seeing her as a patient. It's a strange case and needs someone paying attention to the details, and I don't think your guys are doing that."

Donnie crossed his arms over his large chest and leaned against his chair, thinking. He knew the detectives were lazy, and, if he could do anything about a case, he would do it. "I hate it when you do this to me." He grunted. "What's the name?"

I celebrated with a shriek, giving him a cheesy grin. "Thanks. The girl's name is Bianca Edwards, twenty-two years of age, long wavy strawberry-blond hair, thin, athletic build. Her dad, Ned Edwards, dropped her off at the ortho-pedic center in Illinois yesterday before he went to work.

They scheduled her for a rotator cuff repair procedure, but, when he tried to fetch her that afternoon, nobody at the orthopedic center had any record of her being there. Ever."

"Okay, assuming he's telling us everything, and it's the truth, you'll need to cross reference this with any similar incidents. And when I say you, I'm saying me." He gave a curt nod. "You'll get me fired one of these days."

I grinned at him. "No, I won't. You're too good to get caught."

"What's the doctor's name?"

"Dr. Eltringham. He should be easy to find. He's the only one in our state. I phoned the hospital before coming here, and he only works there Mondays and Tuesdays, and he hasn't been in. Which is weird; it makes my Spidey senses tingle. So, after our meal, I'm heading that way to speak to someone in person, maybe walk around the wards. And if no one there can help me, I'm going to his house."

Donnie narrowed his eyes. "How did you get his home address?"

"Like I said, he's the only Eltringham in Illinois. And I found his address online when I did a quick search." It was a quick backdoor search Billie had added on my work computer, but it only gave me home addresses and nothing else. Billie was our personal tech guy who helped us in obtaining information the police wouldn't otherwise share with us. He helped us gratis, because he knew what we did was for a good cause, and we rarely abused his service.

"Don't, Dana. Rather, wait until I've gone through the case before you see the doctor. If it's an active case, I don't want you anywhere near the doctor, the hospitals, or snooping anywhere. And that includes online."

I sat back and folded my arms, sulking.

"I mean it. I understand the girl's father is desperate to

find her but wait first." He checked his watch. "Sorry, sis. I know it was a short visit, but I've got to go." Donnie stood.

I started to protest, like the spoilt child he knew me to be, until a dark figure entered from outside and stopped in the entranceway, as if they were searching for someone. The sun was still shining brightly into the restaurant, blinding me and casting anyone who stood there in shadows.

Someone in the front screamed.

Donnie spun around, gun drawn.

I was on the ground, one knee up with my gun pointing in the entrance's direction.

The dark figure let off a round, nipping Donnie's shoulder.

He kicked an empty chair in front of him and hit the assailant in the abdomen.

The figure fired another round as the chair hit him, redirecting his aim toward me. The bullet hit the ground and ricocheted into the wall beside me.

I pulled the trigger, shattering glass behind him.

He ran out the way he had entered, with Donnie running after him.

I dashed up and chased after them. Once outside, I panned left and right. I saw Donnie running down the street and followed.

Donnie disappeared into an alley, which I hated; any alley was a breeding ground for the unknown—the drunk homeless, an angry robber, or someone trying to kill us.

As I neared the alley, I skulked around the corner, my gun aiming at anything that might be there.

A figure was on the ground. It was Donnie.

My breath caught in my chest, and all I wanted to do was run to see if he was all right. With my heart thrashing around in my ribs, I sucked in air and slowly exhaled. I needed to ensure the alley was safe; the assailant could be hiding somewhere and jump me as I entered. I focused on Donnie's chest; it was still rising and falling. I didn't see a pool of blood beneath him, but he was injured somehow. I sighed with relief and slowly entered the alley, my eye trained on the dark corners for anything that moved. There was nothing except the gate on the far end of the alley swinging open. He had exited through there and was hopefully gone.

"How badly are you injured, Donnie? Are you hit?" I asked with panic in my tone.

"No." Donnie pushed himself up. "The fucker blindsided me with the wooden beam. He just made me see stars." He glanced at the flesh wound on his shoulder, only noticing it now, and the specks of blood flecked his shirt.

"That doesn't make sense, Donnie. Why shoot at you in the restaurant and then only hit you when he finally had you in the open? Who was this guy, and why was he after you?"

He glared at me. "I can't discuss my cases, sis. You know that. Maybe he just wanted to get my attention or send a warning. Well, he has it now, and my eyes are wide open."

"You gonna be okay?"

"Yeah, I'll be fine." He slung an arm around my shoulder, and we walked out the alley together.

The restaurant owner had called the cops, and Donnie's captain wasn't pleased he had been in the thick of it. We answered questions, and Donnie waited for his captain before we could leave.

"Well, look who's here, Donnie and Dana Mulder," Detective Paul "Lip" Lemming drawled as he neared us. He was offering us his signature pout that gave him his nickname—Lip.

Donnie's demeanor shifted into one I did not want to be on the receiving end of.

I folded my arms.

"Just cause one of you is a failed FBI analyst, while the other is trying to get in, doesn't mean you two is better than us street cops."

Donnie warned me with his eyes.

I wisely stayed silent. Lip always had a way of grating under my skin, and today was no different. Donnie didn't like him much either, but he knew how to handle him. They worked together.

"Don't start, Lip." Donnie shoved two meaty fingers into Lip's chest, who raised his hands in mock surrender.

"Now, now, I'm only pulling your leg." Lip's words were dripping with malice, like blades down my back.

"We need to discuss that missing person case."

"A woman, whatshername?"

"Bianca Edwards."

"She skipped town with her boyfriend, man. Case closed."

"We'll see," Donnie warned.

"You're wasting your time."

"Lip, go be useful somewhere else." Captain Dodd's voice was commanding.

Lip obeyed like a dog whose tail was between his legs. He maneuvered near the restaurant's broken window to ask the owner questions, trying hard to look busy.

"Donnie, you know I hate shit like this. The press will have a field day with this one. And there were kids in the restaurant." Captain Dodd sighed. "Do you know who it was?" He glanced over Donnie's shoulder at his men working the scene. Even though he was speaking with us, he was always alert to everything around him. I suspected his

IQ was off the charts. He always seemed to pick up on everything around him.

"No, Cap, but it could be from my current case."

That caught Captain Dodd's attention. He whipped his head to one side and stared at Donnie. "How so?" He glanced at me and shook his head. "Tell me later. And about this missing person case Lip screwed up"—he stared at Donnie knowingly—"I'm just glad you were here though. This could've been worse. And elections are coming up, Don. Make the arrest swift and clean." He gave a curt nod, shook Donnie's hand, patted him on the shoulder and went to speak with the owner. He had ignored me like I was mud on his shoe.

After Donnie received a pat on the back from his captain, they drilled me with questions and my involvement in the shooting. Everyone knew I was Donnie's sister, yet they still gave me grief. Donnie gave me his *I'm sorry eyes*, chuckled and eventually came to my aid, shooing the nice policewoman away.

"You know, you could've done that much sooner. Now I'll never get those ten minutes back."

He chuckled, and I punched his arm as he walked me to my car.

I climbed in and opened the window, so we could talk.

"I'll call you tonight about your missing woman." He leaned in, going all serious brother on me. "If you see the perp again, Dana, do not approach. Call me, and I will handle it." He arched an eyebrow.

"If I see a scary man dressed in black, I can handle it."

"I know you can, but still. Do. Not. Approach. We don't know what this guy wants or who he works for."

"Thanks for the brotherly love. You know it would be

easier if you just gave me access to your system, then I wouldn't need you to do all the admin."

"As good as you are with data and shooting up shit, you know I can't. But you could always talk to Dodd about joining the team."

We'd had this conversation before. No. Thank. You. I would rather be strapped to a rocket ship and sent into space. I started the engine and waved Donnie away from my window. "You know my answer to that, Donnie. You know I can't."

He tapped the window and pushed away. "I know. Is everything still okay"—he waved hands in the air—"with that?"

"Yeah, I'm good. Thanks. See you Sunday at the parents?"

He held out his fist for me to bump.

I did.

"Yep, and call me if you spot the douche." He tapped the door one last time, then I drove away.

Chapter Five

EVEN THOUGH DONNIE had warned me not to do any snooping, I couldn't help myself. I pulled up to the orthopedic center in Illinois, the same one where Ned had dropped off Bianca yesterday morning. Near the entrance to the right was a small coffee shop for visitors or any patient who wished to prolong the inevitable. On the left was the admissions area where patients with scheduled procedures were admitted. They had a walk-in area for those requiring immediate medical attention with no prior arranged consultation. The area smelled of disinfectant, and a shudder ran through my body. Ever since my hospital stint, I had a thing against all hospitals or medical centers—or doctors in general. They all seemed to have that death *smell*.

Although I had already received information from the hospital stating Bianca had never been admitted here, I wanted to see for myself. I waited patiently in line until it was my turn to speak with the administrative nurse at reception. Her hair was in a tight ponytail, and she wore Coke-bottle glasses. I introduced myself and gave her Bianca's name. She was kind enough to check without me needing any legal documents.

She clicked on the keys and shook her head. "Sorry, but there's no Bianca Edwards scheduled for any procedure nor any consultation." She shrugged and pushed her glasses back up her nose. "Dr. Eltringham works here every Monday where he consults with patients, and Tuesdays he's scheduled to do their procedures if required. As far as I know, this is the only center where he operates. I can either leave him a message to contact you when he can, or you can visit him at the medical center in Aurora." She sat back in her chair, looking a little confused and deflated, like somehow it was her fault they had lost a patient.

If Dr. Eltringham only performed procedures on Tuesdays, why ask Bianca to come on a Monday?

"It's fine. Thanks for your help anyway. Can you tell me whether Dr. Eltringham is booked for any procedures?"

She shook her head. "No. He called in sick, and we had to reschedule all his patients for next week." The lines between her brows furrowed as she continued clicking on the computer.

"What's the matter?" I leaned over the counter to spy her computer screen.

She blinked up at me, her eyes focusing through her glasses, and abruptly switched off her screen. "Perhaps speak with him at his medical center. Let me get you the address."

"Can you give me his phone number as well please?"

"I only have the one at his medical center. He doesn't give out his cell number."

"That's fine. Thanks."

She searched in her drawer for the paper with his

details, jotted down the address and number and handed it over.

"Is there any way I can go to the ward to see if my client is here?" I held up the photo Ned had given me.

She shook her head. "No. Only patients may enter the wards, and visitors during visiting hours. But, if you come back with a court order, we have to give you access."

"Thanks for the address. I'll just go to the bathroom quick before I head out."

She nodded, pointing at the women's bathroom, but remained suspicious.

I tucked the piece of paper into my pocket and headed toward the bathroom across the way and near the coffee shop. Once done, I scanned the area, ensuring nobody was watching me. The nurse I had spoken with earlier was busy with an admission. I saw an orderly pushing a trolley stacked high with bedding; he faced the ground as he pushed. I walked beside him. The bedding blocked my view of the nurse and the security guard who was making his rounds. As we entered the hallway restricted to patients or visitors, the orderly was so busy watching his feet he didn't see me go right toward the wards when he turned left.

Inside the first surgical ward, I stuck in my head and saw two nurses at their station and one walking up and down with a doctor. In the far corner was a girl with auburn hair that shone red in the light. I stepped inside to get a better look until a nurse blocked my view.

"Can I help you?" she demanded in a tone that made me think if I was a patient in her care, I would lie about my recovery just to get out of here and away from her. The nurse had beady brown eyes, dark hair cut short and styled to the back, with fine dark hairs above her top lip. She was also a head taller than me, so I had to look up at her—that alone made me nervous to be around her.

"No, it's okay." I wilted in her shadow and snuck a glance at the girl in the back. As I focused on her, I realized she was a bit older than the girl in the photo Ned had given me. "I got confused. My sister is in the next ward. Thanks anyway."

The nurse accepted my lie and went about her job while I scooped up what was left of my ego and moved on.

The second ward was for men, and the third had two women with strawberry-blond hair, but none of them were Bianca.

As I left the ward, a woman in scrubs approached me and narrowed her eyes suspiciously. We passed one another in the corridor; she stopped to speak with that nurse I had spoken with earlier while I ducked around the corner. I either had to find Bianca or get out before they caught me and had security kick me out. Donnie could only protect me so far; if I got arrested, he would let me sit in jail just to laugh at me later.

Voices echoed, yelling at me to stop.

I ran.

Their footsteps echoed mine.

I ran down another hallway, searching. An exit sign blinked up ahead. I darted for it. I pushed through the doors, and the sun hit me in the eyes. I jumped off the step and sprinted. I hid behind a tree across the parking lot.

That same woman flew out the door with that creepy nurse. Their heads darted left and right, not seeing me. They walked around the parking lot, searched in and under cars and eventually gave up. They walked around the hospital and headed toward the main entrance. The exit door had already closed, and there wasn't a handle on the outside to let them back in.

When it was clear they wouldn't be returning, I strolled to my car.

———

I FOUND a parking spot at the medical center where Dr. Eltringham worked every other day when he wasn't at the orthopedic center. I was the only person there, which was strange for a Tuesday. People were always sick and in need of treatment. I would've assumed the center would remain open with a locum doctor while Dr. Eltringham was ill. A large *Closed* sign hung on the shut glass entrance doors with a note I couldn't read from where I was sitting in my car.

Climbing out the car, I scanned the area again, but it was still only me. I walked to the door to read the note.

Dr. Eltringham is off ill and will be back next week Wednesday. We apologize for any inconvenience. For emergencies, please dial 9-1-1 or go to your nearest medical facility.

I DIDN'T HAVE any other number for the doctor, and, with the center closed, it was no use phoning. I had his home address but not his home phone number. Either Donnie or Billie would have to help with that detail.

But Donnie said it might be an active case, which meant I wasn't allowed to go near the doctor until they had spoken with him. There was nothing left for me to do now but wait —and I hated waiting.

It was after 5 p.m., and I hadn't heard from Marc yet; he was following up on my other client's case, since I now had a new one. I pulled my cellphone from my pocket and punched his number.

"Yoh," Marc answered without me having to hear it ring once. I loved working with him. He was quick, equipped, and efficient.

"How's my client doing?" I asked, watching a man push his cart up the sidewalk.

"I got more pictures. Will print them out and show them to her tomorrow for her nine a.m. appointment. How is our missing case going?"

"Good. Thanks again for helping." I nodded, but Marc couldn't see it.

The homeless man stopped pushing his cart and dug inside a trash can.

"There is no record of the girl at the hospital at all. And the doctor has taken ill. He hasn't been there or at his medical center. Apparently, he'll only be back next week. And Donnie will phone me tonight once he has looked at the case."

"Bummer. So you can't do anything until he gives you confirmation."

"Nope."

The homeless man pulled a red top out the trash.

I needed to see it. I walked toward him. "Listen, I have to go. See you tomorrow."

"Sure, kid."

Returning my cellphone to my pocket, I dashed toward the homeless man who had just thrown the top into his cart and was about to walk away. "Hey, you! Hold up!"

He stared nervously in my direction and pushed his trolley faster.

"Wait! I just want to talk to you." I caught up to him and grabbed his cart to stop it.

"I ain't do nothing."

"I know. I'm not accusing you of anything." I lifted my hands off his cart.

"You a cop?" He narrowed his eyes at me.

"No." I shook my head. "I only want to ask you a couple of questions. The top you just dug out the trash …" I pulled it out his cart and held it up. "Did you see the girl who wore it?" Ned had said Bianca wore a red top, but I wasn't sure whether it was this top.

"No." He shrugged, and the lines between his brows deepened. His eyes glassed over, as if the stress of the questions was too much for him to bear.

"Do you walk by the center often?" I thumbed at the large grey building beside us.

His eyes focused and panned from the building back to me. "Maybe."

"How about two dollars?" I fished the crumpled bill out my pocket and handed it to him. I didn't know if he was stable, high, or playing me to earn free money, or whether he really didn't know anything. Regardless, I would still give him the money even if the information from him proved to be false.

"I come by at least once a day. There's always something good in the trash for me."

"Do they always leave stuff for you to find?"

He nodded.

"Have you seen anything out of the ordinary?"

He shook his head.

"Has anything happened here? Maybe shouting? Or an angry patient storming out the center?"

He shook his head. "I ain't never seen the doctor, if

that's what you wanna know. I seen the nurse. She's the one who gives me stuff."

"Oh, can you tell me about her? Describe her." I pulled my notebook and pen from my back pocket.

"She's real pretty. Has long blond hair, but she always has it in a bun. It looks too tight on her face." He paused, deep in thought. "And she feeds me. Leaves day-old food. She knows I'm always hungry, but she feeds me. I come by every day this time. But today, there's no one. They closed."

I made my notes and thanked him. "Can I keep this top?"

He shook his head and tore it from my hands. "No, no, no—"

"I think this belongs to a client of mine," I whispered, keeping my voice as calm as possible.

He seemed spooked.

"She went missing yesterday. You didn't see a girl wearing this top?" I repeated the question.

His eyes widened, and he released the top as if it stung him.

I picked it up and held it higher to check for any marks or holes. There were none.

"I don't know about a girl." He swallowed hard.

"What's your name?"

He pursed his lips.

"So I know who to call when I come by with some things."

His shoulders sagged, and he physically relaxed. "Oh. Abe. You can call me Abe." He smiled, revealing gaps where his top and bottom front teeth were meant to be; the rest of his teeth were stained brown.

"Hi, Abe. My name is Dana. Would it be okay if I come

back in a few days' time to speak with you? Maybe you'll remember something by then."

He nodded shyly.

"Great, thanks. Meanwhile, would you mind keeping an eye on this place for me?"

"For what?" He glanced back at the grey center.

"Anything at all, anything you think seems a little different." I felt in my other back pocket, removed another crumpled bill and handed it to him. "Get yourself something to eat. No alcohol, Abe. Some food."

His face beamed when he saw the twenty. "Yes, ma'am." He grabbed the bill from my hand and pushed his cart down the street, heading toward the corner store.

Chapter Six

THEY WERE the only Eltringhams in the entire state of Illinois, so I was quite certain it was the address for the doctor. I parked across the street to their lavish home—the long driveway leading to the newly painted white walls, dark grey exterior window shutters, and a hand-carved mahogany front door. The double wooden garage door was off to the side, and the home boasted double stories with an attic, making it almost three stories high. In the attic window, I saw a blonde woman reach for a book from a shelf. A man entered behind her, took the book out her hand and gave her a different book.

Donnie warned me not to speak with the doctor, but their house was on my way home anyway. I only wanted to ask a few questions.

Using the lion head knocker on the door once, it was loud enough to alert them to my presence. I heard quick footsteps down the stairs, and the woman abruptly opened the door.

"Can I help you?" she asked with confusion on her face,

as if they never received visitors. She checked her watch, emphasizing I may have interrupted them.

"Mrs. Eltringham?"

"Yes?"

"Is this where Dr. Eltringham lives?"

"Yes." She closed the door slightly, so I no longer had view of the stairs.

"My name is Dana Mulder. I'm a private investigator and would like to ask you a few questions regarding Dr. Eltringham's patients. May I come in?"

"No, you may not." She stepped closer and inched the door closed.

"Can I speak with Dr. Eltringham?"

"No, he is ill. I'll speak on his behalf." She spoke clearly but softly so only I could hear. "We're not allowed to divulge patient information—"

I raised my hand to stop her from carrying on. I did not want patient information. I already knew who the patient was. "I only want to know whether you're aware that one of Dr. Eltringham's patients is missing, and I'd like to know if you know anything." Even though the hospital had already informed me that no patient by that name had been admitted, I wanted to see whether Mrs. Eltringham knew anything about Bianca.

"Alright, which patient?"

"Bianca Edwards."

She slowly shook her head from side to side, her eyes cast downward and to the side, as if recalling information. "No, nope. Bianca Edwards you say?"

I nodded.

"Nope. I don't recall a patient with that name come into the medical center. Are you sure it's one of our patients?"

Her frown was back, and she almost looked concerned. Almost.

"Yes. Her father said she saw Dr. Eltringham, and, unless I'm mistaken, there is only one Eltringham."

"You are correct. He is the only one, but we did not see this girl. Dr. Eltringham is off sick this week, so it's not him. I'm sorry, but I have to go." She stepped backward into the foyer.

I was quick enough and stuck my foot between the door and the doorjamb in case she wanted to close the door in my face without replying to my question.

"Who is it, Mary?" Dr. Eltringham called from upstairs.

"It's okay, honey. She was just leaving!" Her eyes widened when she noticed I had moved closer to her.

"Please. Her father is adamant it's Dr. Eltringham."

"I'm sorry, but the father is mistaken. I help in the medical center and no such patient was ever there."

If the doctor and his good wife had something to do with Bianca's disappearance, it was no use trying to get information from them. They would continue denying everything. I needed to stay in their good graces, so I could question them again without having the police present. I would prefer to speak directly with the doctor, but, since his gatekeeper was blocking me and had already answered my questions, it would be difficult to continue questioning unless I had new information to work with. And besides, Donnie had instructed me not to see them. I didn't want to anger them and have them call the cops on me.

I plastered on a fake smile. "I will check with the father again. Sorry for troubling you. Thank you for your time, Mrs. Eltringham."

"Sure, no problem. Good luck." She closed the door in my face.

I walked down their long driveway toward my car and dialed Ned's number as I climbed into the driver's seat. "Hi, Ned?"

"Who's this?"

"Dana."

"Oh, right—"

"I don't suppose you have any proof that Bianca was at the medical center?"

"I have a receipt for a consultation. Would that help? We prefer to pay up front and file a claim with the insurance company."

"That's perfect. Could I pick it up? I've got a red top to show you."

Chapter Seven

CHEWING on a mouthful of beef chow mein, I pressed keys on my laptop then waited for the search results. Nothing. In the public domain, no other patient or women of similar age or appearance to Bianca had gone missing. I needed that info from Donnie whenever he decided to call, or I needed to call Billie—he would do the search for me.

I sipped on my beer while I browsed. The liquid was already warm, but I finished it anyway while contemplating what to search for next; social media always sprung to mind —the next best thing for sleuths.

My online presence was that of a ghost; my profile pictures consisted of an animated avatar. The profile was set to private and no one was allowed to contact me or ask to be my *friend*. The friends I had were ghosts I had created. I cringed every time I browsed these sites; some people were too eager to share their personal information, and my blood boiled when they showed pictures of their children. Predators did not discriminate, only that their victims were under a certain age.

I pressed keys and opened four tabs for each of the various websites and searched for Bianca Edwards. I got four hits on the first social media site and clicked the one I was looking for. Problem number one: her account was not private, so any Tom, Dick, or Harry could view her having drinks at this bar, visiting friends here, vacationing there, and when she was at work—and worse, where she worked. All addresses were visible because of check-ins, along with other personal information—which was important information to a psychopath, stalker, marketing or government agency to name a few. All of it was priceless data, and, depending on how it was to be used, could either be lethal or someone was about to make a lot of money.

I wanted to learn who her friends were, where she frequented, with whom, how often, and why. It could either lead me to who had kidnapped her, or it could all be useless information, and she was taken because it was an opportunity the perpetrator couldn't let pass by.

I scrolled through her pages on all four platforms for hours. My eyes were burning by the time it was midnight, and exhaustion had taken over. But I now knew who her close friends were and that her dad was never featured in any of her pictures—either he didn't have an account, or he didn't like having his picture taken. I knew where she worked, the times she worked, and where she enjoyed vacationing. The pictures of her food and the check-ins of the various restaurants revealed her favorite places to eat and how often she visited. There was one picture of a guy where he had replied to a comment and had liked the post. But he was never mentioned again. That had happened a week ago. This guy had deleted his account sometime thereafter. I made copious amounts of notes that I could share with Donnie if he ever phoned.

I flinched when my cell rang. "What?" I barked into the receiver.

"Do you want the information or not?"

"Of course, but why are you only phoning me now?"

"Stop being a cry baby, or I'm going to tell Mom." Donnie chuckled. "Okay, your missing person is an administrator for a telecommunications company." That confirmed my social media search. "She's never had a fine or any arrests. She seems like a good kid. Her dad owns a construction company, has had two parking tickets, and owns a house here and a summer home in Florida. And Dr. Eltringham has had a few complaints against him."

"Wait, let me get my pen." I reached for the pen I had thrown across my dining table in frustrated exhaustion before Donnie had called. "Okay, go." I stifled a yawn.

"He prescribed the wrong medicine or knowingly prescribed controlled substances. One case, he failed to diagnose a medical problem that was later found. Then he failed to provide the appropriate post-operative care or respond to a call from a hospital to help a patient in a traumatic situation. All this happened last year. Unfortunately, all the complaints were dismissed."

"What happened last year to cause the doctor to make so many mistakes? And how can so many cases be dismissed like that?" I knew the answer to the second question, yet I still asked out of annoyance for the system or lack thereof.

"Not sure what happened, but I suspect it all caught up with him last year, whatever it was. But you're welcome to ask the state medical board why they dropped the cases. If I had to guess, they were most likely lacking in the evidence department or the witnesses withdrew their testimony."

Which I was sure happened often. "Did any of his patients disappear?"

I heard him rustled through papers. "I could only find one who disappeared last year. Rosemary Haynes. Her boyfriend Todd Williams listed her as missing, but her parents stated she would do that at least once a year: leave for a week or two then return home. The boyfriend wasn't convinced though. Unfortunately, the case wasn't followed up, and we don't know if she returned home or not."

"Who worked the case?"

"The other two," he replied, referring to Stuart and Lip; their lack of investigating cases was becoming a habit.

"Okay. Thanks, bro. Can you give me the address?"

"Since this happened last year and might not be related to our current case, I'll give it to you."

I jotted down the address and the names of Rosemary's parents and her boyfriend. "What did you find out about Bianca?"

"Lip opened the investigation. He called the doctor and the hospital and wrote down that neither knew the missing person. No other witnesses or clues to her whereabouts. It frustrates me that he isn't pursuing this and hasn't bothered to do much of anything else."

"Now what?"

"I've told Dodd, and I'm taking over the case. I will do my best to prioritize this one with my current case load and will bring in James and another officer."

"Sounds good." I was silent for a heartbeat. "Don't yell at me, but ..."

"What did you do?"

"Nothing, I swear. But I did stop by their medical center. It's closed, and I found a red top in the trash. Her dad says it's hers, and he has a receipt showing she was there."

"Okay, noted. Don't go there again, Dana."

"I promise. Can I continue with my case?"

"Allow us to start over with the investigation, then you can start your prodding."

"But I can still look into Rosemary?" I flinched in anticipation.

"I already said you could. It's not an active case. And besides, I think this case needs all hands, and I would rather have you on board than the others." Again, referring to the other two investigators. They were the only two detectives I'd come across who sucked wholeheartedly at their job.

"Okay, and you will share with me what you find?"

He chuckled. "Sure, but only if you share with me what you find."

I smiled. "Yes. Anything else?"

"Just be careful, that's all."

"I will." I sounded like an angry, spoiled child. "I've done this for a few years now. You don't have to keep treating me like a kid anymore."

He sighed. He was my brother and always looked out for me; it was part of his DNA. "And how are you after this afternoon's incident?"

"I'm fine, I promise." And I was. I had experienced a shooting once or twice, or ten times in my career. I was sure Donnie had already stopped counting the number of times he had to defend himself or shoot a bad guy.

"You sure?" he asked carefully, like he was walking on shards of glass around me.

"Yeah, big brother. I'm fine." I didn't like being treated like a frightened child all the time. I had one incident. One. It happened four years ago. And since then, he's always asking about my wellbeing. Besides, I already saw a shrink, I didn't need another one.

"Call me the moment you find anything on Rosemary

and if you think the cases are connected." He was quiet for a heartbeat. "And, sis?"

"Yeah."

"Call me for anything."

"Thanks, but I'm fine. You're wasting your energy on the wrong person. I promise. I'm up early tomorrow, so I need to get some sleep. And thanks for the info."

"Sure."

We said bye. I placed my cellphone on the table and closed my laptop. In the kitchen, I had a swig or two of the open bottle of wine. My stomach rumbled, but I didn't want to eat a meal before bed. I proceeded to rummage through the cupboards, but I was fresh out of chocolates. My late-night snacking was evident, and it left my cupboards bare. I needed to buy groceries. I couldn't keep buying takeout; it was bad for my waistline.

I readied for bed and placed my Glock in its holder against my headboard and climbed under the covers. Eyeing the clock on my cell now charging on my bedside table, I would have about six hours of uninterrupted sleep and couldn't wait a second longer. I switched off my lamp, bathing me in darkness, and allowed Mr. Sandman to take me away.

The waterfall was magnificent as the moon reflected a mercury shine. The water stopped flowing, but a continuous dripping remained.

Drip. Drip. Drip.

I jackknifed out of bed, grabbed my Glock out of habit and trained one half-open, blurry eye on my bathroom door, which was ajar, and the light was on. I always slept with the lights off. All of them.

Movement caught my eye. I spun to the right toward the

window. The curtain moved again, revealing the wide-open window.

Drip. Drip. Drip.

I swiveled my arm to the left toward the bathroom door and waited, listening. There was nothing else, no other sounds apart from the water dripping in the basin and the wind outside. Climbing out of bed, my eyes had adjusted to the hallway's darkness and could see well enough. When I was comfortable no one was there, I pushed open the bathroom door with my foot. It was empty, but the basin was full of water and almost overflowing onto the floor. The tap was open slightly, so only a drop of water fell at a time.

Drip. Drip. Drip.

That was not me. I would never do this.

Someone was here.

Someone had entered my house to taunt me, to scare me.

———

ALL THE LIGHTS WERE ON, and Donnie paced throughout the house. It was 5 a.m. when I had called him; he had been up anyway and said he would be right over. Now he was trudging his muddy boots on my clean carpet, checking that the windows were bolted down.

"You need to install an alarm, Dana." The lines between his eyes deepened, his mouth in a tight line. It was cool, yet beads of sweat dripped down the sides of his face. He had trampled my garden to shreds, looking for signs of whoever had broken in and left evidence, but there weren't any—not even footprints. It was like they had opened my window and flew in.

"Why, when I have you?" I attempted a grin, but Donnie's face was a warning not to test him this morning.

"This isn't a joke, Dana. Whoever it was could've hurt you. Or worse."

That sobered me up, and I glanced at my feet like a scolded child. "I know, but they didn't hurt me. It was a warning."

"This time, Dana. They didn't do anything *this time*." He punctuated his words with the hard, cold reality. "We've kept you safe for four years, Dana. What if he found you?"

I fell onto my bed, eyes misty, but I refused to let it get to me. I wouldn't allow anyone or any case affect me. Never again.

"It's not—"

"No," I interrupted. "It's been four years. Why would they start up now again? Out of nowhere."

He exhaled audibly. He didn't believe me but didn't call me out on it.

I didn't think it was them. *Him*. It couldn't be. It was my one and only case I had worked on while at the FBI. I had been fresh out of the academy, eager to please and determined to put the psychopaths behind bars. I'd figured out the pattern they had used to dump the bodies, but they had proved better than us. They had killed three agents in a blink of an eye and beat on the fourth so badly he was currently on disability. *He* had sliced me up pretty badly, and I had been in the hospital for a couple of days.

I folded my arms. As stubborn as I was, my brother knew me better.

"Promise me"—he pulled me into a hug—"if it is him, you will tell me."

I nodded into his chest. "Thanks, but I don't think it's

him. And, even if it was, I have no idea where he is to even do anything. He could just be toying with me."

He let go and went to the bathroom to wash his hands.

I noticed my muddy shoulders. "What did you do to my garden? You've managed to get mud all over my carpet and now on me."

"Investigating," he chimed from the bathroom. "Do you want to come in to give us your statement? I can call in the guys to fingerprint your place."

It was my turn to sigh. "Fine, but I need to be quick. We have a client coming in at nine a.m."

"You will be done by then."

Chapter Eight

"AN OFFICER COULDN'T HAVE TAKEN my statement?" I swiveled the chair to face Donnie. His new partner, Detective James Michaels, had just stepped out of the office to fetch forms from the front office.

"I want someone I trust and who's impartial to investigate this, Dana." He tapped keys on his keyboard without glancing at me.

"Right, where were we?"

I flinched as James entered their shared office. His voice was deep and throaty and matched his dark demeanor. My first impression of him: the quiet and shy type, with the possibility of having a violent streak. My mother always warned me against those types. But, so far, I was right on the first two only; he hadn't displayed any violence—yet. I'd met him the first month they had partnered up when Donnie had brought him over for Sunday lunch at the parents' house. Since then, he'd joined us for lunch a few times. He was easy to talk to once he started talking. His chestnut-colored hair was shaved neatly on the sides, the top long but out of his face to highlight his honey-colored eyes.

James smirked when he sat; he'd seen me jump upon his arrival. Somehow, I was amusing to him as much as I was to my brother.

"Do you want to start from the beginning?"

There wasn't much of a beginning. I told him how someone had entered my house and opened the bathroom tap and left it running. Story over.

"No, not that beginning." He watched me suspiciously. "From four years ago."

I groaned inwardly. "Fine." I crossed my arms as I leered at Donnie. "T'was a dark and stormy night—"

Donnie flicked my shoulder.

"Ow, you brute." I rubbed the spot he had flicked until the burning stopped.

"Take this seriously, Dana," Donnie grumbled. "All of it."

"Fine." I groaned. "It was my first month with the agency here in Chicago. Murders were happening all over the city, with all different MOs. At first glance, one would think each case was different, not related at all. But the more I investigated them, the more I suspected they were eerily similar. Even though the vic's had been murdered in strange, horrific ways and with different weapons, we suspected it was the same killers. We were stuck, not knowing what was going on, until I figured out the pattern that connected them—"

"Which was?" James interrupted me.

"Do you want the story or not?"

He nodded.

"Then leave me to talk uninterrupted."

He sat back in his chair but kept his meaty arm on the

desk, so he could write my statement, allowing me to continue.

"All the victims had priors or had been arrested on suspicion of murder and somehow released back into society. We should've been happy someone was taking out the trash. But murder is murder, no matter who was doing it or why. These vigilantes were at least six people, that we knew of, because of the different murder weapons used and that they were each used so differently. One perp was left-handed, the rest right. One liked to carve, one liked to use a bow and arrow, one a shotgun—you know, that kind of thing." I swallowed hard at the memory.

James gave me a moment to gather my thoughts—of the attack and the nightmares that followed. And the therapy I'd been skipping. When I didn't answer, James spoke. "What happened next?" he prompted in a delicate whisper, treading lightly, as if I was about to bolt out the office.

I glanced up at him and suppressed the flashes of bodies lying on the ground and the blood. So much blood. It was a slaughter. "I focused on the days of the dumps and the areas where they had dumped the previous victims and anticipated where they would drop the next one. I proposed three spots where I thought the killers might dump the next body and on which night. The agent in charge actually listened to me. Normally, analysts wouldn't go into the field, but I asked, and they agreed. I already had the training, so I was ready and wanted to be there when they nabbed the killers. I stayed in the car while the agents hid in the surrounding area. And do you know what?" I asked rhetorically with a smirk. "They came to the spot where we waited. They dropped the body, and, before they left, the agents sprang on them. There were six of them and four agents, while I stayed in a car. When three agents went down, I climbed out the car to help. I stopped them from killing the fourth agent, but they injured me. They wore masks of various animals, so their faces weren't visible. The one with the mask of a pig hovered over me while I was bleeding and told me to stay down or I would die. I stayed down, and they left." I swallowed hard. "They left the agent and me alive. I met Marc at the hospital, and he offered me a job I couldn't refuse, and I left the FBI." I studied James, waiting for that spark of disappointment I usually saw in colleagues' faces. But James only wore an expression of concern. It was refreshing.

"Did they try to contact you afterward?" James stopped writing. His gaze flitted from mine to Donnie's then back to me. He already knew the answer, yet he wanted me to say it anyway.

"A year later, to the hour, they left a pig mask in front of my apartment door. When I answered the knock, I saw the mask. The cameras revealed no one coming in or out of the building, like it had been a ghost. One moment, there was nothing; the next moment, there's the mask." What I didn't say was since that day it felt like someone was watching me around every corner. If I had said anything to Donnie, he would've had me in a safehouse, which I wasn't prepared to do. My arms pebbled. "The next day, Donnie helped me move into another apartment under a different name, and five months later, I moved again, and continued doing that until I bought my current house under my aunt's name."

James arched an eyebrow. "It's possible they know where you live now."

I shrugged. "Maybe, I don't know. I haven't heard from them since they left that mask."

James set down his pen and sipped his coffee. "The

techs might be done with your house. We'll know in a few days whether anyone besides you and your brother were there."

I stood.

"Sign here before you go, please." Maybe it was the *please* or his politeness, but I signed the document after scanning through it.

"Is there anything else?"

"Do you have somewhere else you can stay?" James glanced at Donnie again, as if they'd had a private discussion about what to do with me before I had arrived to give my statement.

"I'm not hiding. If I stay with someone, then whoever is doing this will know where that person lives. I won't put their life in danger for mine. I'll stay at my place. I'm not afraid." Who was I fooling? I was afraid, but I'd be damned if I got someone else killed because of them; I had watched these monsters kill three agents in cold blood, with one hanging on for dear life—I wouldn't be watching again.

James pursed his lips. He either didn't agree with my option or he thought I was stubborn—or both. But I didn't know the man that well nor did I care.

Donnie frowned at me then eyed the papers on his desk. "Then I'm staying by you." He looked up; his penetrating blue eyes gave me no option.

"No, brother." I shook my head. "I cannot let you do that. Madeline and the boys won't like it. It's stressful enough for them that you're always on the job, now you must look after your kid sister. You won't be babysitting me. I refuse. I'll call you if anything happens, again."

He started mumbling something, but I lifted my hand to stop him. "I'll install an alarm."

Donnie stood and towered over me. If I wasn't his sister

or knew him very well, his size alone would intimidate me. He looked after himself and kept in shape. He constantly carried on about having a healthy body and healthy mind. His cold stare had thawed somewhat, only a smidge, but he was still unhappy.

I couldn't and wouldn't allow him to put his life in danger. I loved his kids, all three boys; the youngest was only three while the eldest being thirteen. They still needed their father. I didn't have any kids or anyone; it was just me. I could afford to lose if that's what it came down to.

"I need to get to work." I hugged Donnie, "Thanks for taking my statement, James. Will you let me know if you find any usable fingerprints?"

"Yeah, sure," he mumbled, sounding just like Donnie. No wonder Captain Dodd put them together; they were painfully the same.

Chapter Nine

I SWIRLED the black sludge in my mug; the stirrer moved around and around with the momentum. When I had arrived at work, they had already made the coffee. I cursed under my breath as I sipped the liquid and had the urge to throw it out and start over again, but my client was about to arrive.

"It won't kill you," Nigel, the other PI in Marc's company, chirped from around the corner. Marc had worked with Nigel for years before I started, and, since Nigel was covert, they didn't tell me how they had met or where they used to work or what they did. I knew Marc was a Navy Seal and surmised that was where he and Nigel had first started their professional relationship. They never told me what Nigel did for the business or the type of cases he worked on. But that didn't mean I couldn't tease him about his awful coffee.

"One day, it might, Nigel. Your coffee always tastes burnt and is a little thick. What do you add to it anyway? Mud?"

"Ha, you're funny. No, I don't add anything. I might add one or two extra spoons of coffee, but that's it." He entered the kitchen and poured himself a cup and added creamer and four spoons of brown sugar.

"Well, if the coffee doesn't kill you, the sugar will."

"Stay outta my business, woman," he replied in a playful groan then grinned. His teeth were perfect and white, a contrast to his unkept scruffy mousy hair and wrinkled clothing.

"Where did you sleep last night?" I took a step backward. He didn't smell very fresh either.

"That is none of your business."

"Your clothing, Nigel, and your hair. What's going on with you today?" I waved my hand at his head and body for effect.

"It's called investigating, darling."

"What case are you working on? The homeless?"

"You know I can't tell you." He sipped from his mug and patted me on the head like one would a dog.

I swatted his hand before he could pat me a second time. "Next time, I'm gonna shoot your hand if you touch me like that again."

"Sorry"—he raised his hand in surrender—"but you're like my kid sister. Can I give you a hug?"

"No thanks." I left the kitchen before he could pin me down for a hug.

The doorbell chimed, and my nine o'clock entered our office.

Marc glanced up from his laptop, his jaw slack.

Mrs. Jackson stopped near my desk.

"Dana, so good to see you again." I motioned for her to sit.

Marc was still staring at her.

I ignored him. "Sorry I couldn't take your call yesterday. We had a walk-in I was speaking with. You've met Marc?"

Mrs. Jackson seemed to only realize then someone else was in the office with us and smiled at Marc—a smile that could cause any man's pants to shrink in the front.

I think Marc was drooling. He stood from his chair, kicked the desk leg and almost fell. With his arm extended, she shook his hand. He cupped her hand with both of his.

I arched an eyebrow at him. I'd never seen him do that before—it was very gentlemanly. I guessed there was a first for everything. Then again, I couldn't blame him; Mrs. Jackson was stunning. She used to model when she was younger, but I didn't think she looked a day over thirty—she was forty-eight.

"Nice to meet you." She smiled again, leaving Marc with a stupid gaga expression. "It was you I spoke with?"

Marc nodded. I think he swallowed his tongue.

I stifled a laugh and interrupted their moment. "Thanks for coming in. Marc got more photos for your case, Mrs. Jackson."

Marc was still holding her hand.

"Marc?" I scolded.

He glanced at me; his eyes glazed over with her beauty still etched in his periphery.

"Would you mind getting the pictures?"

"Oh, yeah, sure." He finally released her hand and fetched the photos from his desk drawer. He returned and sat in the chair beside hers.

I rolled my eyes and was glad no one saw me.

Marc reviewed the photos. "As you can see, your suspicions were on par. We took photos last week and again yesterday, and it's the same woman. A background check revealed that she works at the nudie bar on Main Road.

She's single and supports a three-year-old." Marc became quiet to let it all sink in while Mrs. Jackson perused the photos on her own.

Mrs. Jackson finally looked up, eyes misty, a little paler than when she had first arrived, and cleared her throat. "Thank you. Do you know whether the kid is his? He looks just like him." She held up a photo of the little boy. His sandy-brown hair matched her husband's, along with his husky-blue eyes.

"We've submitted a paternity test, and the results should be available next week," I confirmed.

"I don't want to know how you got the samples." She grabbed a tissue from her bag and blew her nose.

"We are discreet, Mrs. Jackson. No one would suspect anything. Nor would any of it come back to you." I pushed the box of tissues closer to her in case she didn't have more in her bag.

"Thank you." She threw her used tissue into the trash can. "You don't mind if I keep these?" She held up the photos.

I opened my mouth to respond.

"They're all yours," Marc added before I could answer.

I would speak with him once our client left. "Correct, these are your copies. If you want more, we can print them for you."

Mrs. Jackson nodded. "I'll give them to my lawyer. He'll be in touch if he needs anything else from you." She stood. "How much do I still owe you?"

I motioned to the receptionist desk where the card machine was and handed her the final invoice.

She gave me the balance in cash, folded the invoice with manicured hands and tucked it into the expensive bag she was clutching onto for dear life.

I suspected we were the cause of her instant instability with the proof of her husband's infidelity, but her lawyer would be expensive enough to ensure she'd have a fair divorce that leaned more to her side.

Once she had left, I opened the strategically placed wall safe behind a painting at the back of the office, placed the cash in an envelope and on top of the rest then turned to Marc. "You can close your mouth now." I winked and sat behind my desk again.

Nigel chose that moment to enter the open-plan office and sat at his desk.

Marc scowled silently, sat in his chair again and tapped on his laptop keys, avoiding eye contact.

"She sure is pretty," Nigel cooed from his desk.

"Shut up," Marc barked without looking at any of us.

"She'll be divorced soon, Marc, then you can tap that ass," I teased.

Marc ignored me and continued onto business. "What's happening with our missing girl from yesterday?"

I gave them an update about Dr. Eltringham, that he had taken ill and that his center was closed until next week —and that it was an active case, and I couldn't go near him, again, but they didn't have to know that part.

"What are you doing today? And did the father pay his deposit?"

"Not yet, but he said he'd swing by later for an update. And Donnie gave me a lead I want to check out first."

Chapter Ten

THE DOOR OPENED the second time I rang the bell. A woman answered wearing a gown and loose hair curlers. She squinted while glancing up and down my body.

I had the urge to cover up even though I was wearing jeans, a blouse, and a jacket. "Mrs. Haynes?" I plastered my best smile across my face.

"Yes? What do *you* want?"

"My name is Dana Mulder. I'm a private investigator, and I'd like to speak with you."

"Why?" She kept her hand on the handle of the screen door but kept it closed.

"It concerns your daughter Rosemary."

Mrs. Haynes unlocked the screen door and fumbled with the handle to pull it open. "My daughter? Have you found her? Please come in." She stood to one side, allowing me entry.

Boxes lined against the wall and floor. On top of the boxes were bags spewing old, dirty clothing. Hangers protruded from other boxes, and I noticed some contained magazines dating back to last year.

"Watch your step." Mrs. Haynes pointed at a stack of magazines near my feet. She locked the door behind me and led the way through a path lined with junk.

A cockroach scattered past with tiny ones following it. The hairs on the back of my neck rose, and my arms pebbled. The distinct smell of smoke, mold, dusty clothing, and feces assaulted my nose the farther we entered the bowels of her living room—I assumed; I had no idea what type of room it was, since it was filled with junk. The curtains were drawn—the sun trying its best to enter, but the thick smoke hung in the air with sparkly dust particles dancing near my face. I had to stop myself from covering my mouth and nose then realized too late that opting to breathe through my mouth was a bad mistake.

She pushed an old pizza box from the couch to the floor and pointed for me to sit.

I remained standing. A darker mark on the couch made it look damp. I shuddered. "I shouldn't be taking up much of your time, Mrs. Haynes. It is in connection with your daughter. From what you just said, I gather she hasn't returned home since last year after you reported her missing."

She shook her head; her eyes held unshed tears. "Todd knew she was gone, but we didn't listen. She had disappeared before, but then she came back home. She always returned. And we thought it was like those times. We didn't think she was gone forever." The waterworks exploded, and it was messy—snot, tears, and regret. She yanked an old shirt from a box and blew her nose.

I gagged. "When did you realize she wasn't coming back?"

My question broke her crying fit. She wiped her face dry, red cheeks blossomed, and her eyes glistened in the dim light. "My husband kept saying she would be back, to give her one more month and she will be back. We just had to wait. She always returned. But when four months passed and unanswered phone calls, I knew she was gone. My husband was in denial, so I chased him out the house. I went back to the police station with Todd, and we filled in a new missing report. That was eight months ago, and we still haven't heard from anyone. Until you." A rogue tear slid down her cheek. Her complexion was paler than when I had first arrived.

If she had filed a new report, Donnie would've found it; perhaps it was mislabeled.

"Who helped you? Can you remember the officer's name?" I took my notebook from my back pocket.

"Uh ..." She frowned. "No, I'm sorry." Her frown left her forehead, and her eyes lit up, as if she thought of something. "Why have you come here if you don't have any information on my daughter?" The hardness I had first seen in her eyes when I knocked on her door was back.

"Your daughter disappeared when she was scheduled to have a procedure. Is that correct?"

She nodded.

I took it as my cue to continue. "I discovered your daughter's file during my investigation of another case with similar circumstances. I needed to find out if Rosemary had come home."

"I see. So the doctor has done it again?" she asked, her face stoic.

"Which doctor are you referring to?"

"Dr. Eltringham."

"Did you see or speak with him at all when your daughter disappeared?"

"We tried once, but that nurse kept preventing us." She closed her eyes, thinking or recalling a memory. "She had blond hair and was about your height. We went to the family center where he works, because the orthopedic center doesn't allow you in if you don't have an appointment or are there to see a patient. They are very strict." As if the news was too much, she sat on the dark spot on the couch, and I couldn't be sure if it was damp or not. She didn't seem to mind if it was damp.

"Can you remember which procedure Rosemary was scheduled for? And do you have a picture of her I can keep?"

"She hurt her shoulder, or rather someone hit her, and the old injury flared up. But it was worse this time around. At first, we thought it was whiplash, but then she complained about her entire shoulder, with pain shooting down her arm. They recommended this doctor." She rose from the couch, pulled a photo album from under a box and paged through it. "You can have this one. It's one of the more recent ones." She handed me the picture. "She was so happy there."

I noticed Rosemary's emerald-colored green eyes first. She too had shoulder-length, straight strawberry-blond hair. Freckles littered her cream-colored complexion. She was at a birthday party; her mom and dad were in the picture, with a boy in the background. I felt blood drain from my face. It felt like an ice bucket had been thrown over me. I had seen this boy before; he was in one of Bianca's social media pictures.

I pointed to him and tapped his face with my short nail. "Do you know who that is?"

"That's Todd. They were together about a year before she went missing."

Chapter Eleven

I THANKED MRS. HAYNES, promised to contact her if I found information about her daughter.

These two cases were connected, and I needed to speak with Todd; he had known both victims before they disappeared. Mrs. Haynes said she hadn't seen Todd the last eight months. When Mr. Haynes moved out, Todd stopped visiting her.

I'd only seen Todd in one photo with Bianca, where he commented he loved her hair. Since then, his account was closed, and that was the only *like* and comment he had posted. If he was dating Bianca, no other evidence pointed to it.

Before I could see Todd, I had a meeting with Ned to review what I had discovered. I would ask him whether he knew Todd. But before I did any of that, I needed to speak with Donnie. I thumbed my cellphone and dialed his number.

"Yoh," he barked.

"Jeez, can you ever greet someone like a human being?"

"No. Now what do you want? I'm kinda busy here." He chewed loudly. He was disgusting.

"What are you eating?" I climbed into my car and started the engine.

"Fries. Now speak before I hang up on you."

"I just spoke with Mrs. Haynes, Rosemary's mom."

A *hmmm* sound came from him between mouthfuls of fries.

"Remember you mentioned last night the boy who accompanied Rosemary's parents after she went missing. Did the file have anything else on him? And, can you give me his last known address? Mrs. Haynes doesn't remember where he lives." I gave him a short version of my visit with Rosemary's mother and how I think Todd may be connected to the two cases.

"I don't like this." He sighed.

"I'm not a rookie. I know what I'm doing," I said in a growl into my hands-free kit and reversed out onto the road. "Give me his address, so I can question him."

"Dana, if Todd is connected to our current case, that means you cannot visit him."

"I'm right here, Donnie. It'll be a quick conversation, and I'll phone you the moment I'm done. What do you say?"

He sighed audibly. "Hold on …" I heard him slapping keys on his keyboard, followed by licking sounds.

"Are you sucking your fingers?"

"Uh-huh, you should try these fries. They're so good."

"Maybe later."

"Okay, here we go." Donnie gave me the address, which I entered into my GPS. His house was a few blocks from the Haynes' residence.

I thanked him and hung up. When I checked where

Ned's house was, I found it was only four blocks on the other side of Todd's, who was in the middle of the two houses. It was suspiciously convenient that Todd's house was between the two missing women's houses. Did the two women know one another? Or was Todd the only common thread?

Since Todd's house was closest— it had been his parents' home before they died in a car accident five years ago—I went there first before my meeting with Ned and parked across the street. Todd Williams was twenty-nine and, as the owner of his dad's printing company, managed it from the comfort of his couch. That's what Donnie had on their system. Whether it was still true, I would have to see for myself. I walked across the street toward his front door.

A meow caught me off guard. A chocolate-brown cat with light brown spots rubbed its furry body against my leg. It looked like someone had splashed acid on the cat, lightening the dark brown fur in splotches. He lifted his head, and Sauron-like eyes pierced my soul. I was dumbstruck for a moment, the cat's fiery stare hypnotizing me—waiting for the Dark Lord to send me back to wherever he wanted to send me. The slit of the cat's pupil was dark and soulless.

I was so engrossed with the exotic feline I didn't hear the front door open. I flinched when a man's voice sounded behind me.

"Beautiful, isn't he?"

Standing slowly, I came face to face with the man from the photos—my height, baby-blue eyes, and brown bed hair. His wore jeans, a black t-shirt, and a jacket. He stood barefoot, not affected by the cool air. "Todd?"

He nodded. "Yes, and you are?" He proffered a hand, which I shook.

"Dana Mulder."

He was about to comment when I quickly added, "No relation to the TV show."

He grinned.

"Did I come at a bad time?"

"No. I heard you talking to Felix." He picked up his unusual-looking cat.

Felix pressed his paws against Todd's chest, lifting his chin for a scratch.

"I'm a private investigator and would like to ask you a couple questions, if you don't mind." I watched Todd's reaction for anything out of the ordinary, but so far, his behavior was normal.

He arched an eyebrow but continued tickling his cat behind the ear. "Private investigator? What's this about?" The lines between his brows furrowed.

"A missing girl."

"Would you like to come in?"

Glancing over his shoulder, I noticed the inside of his house was neat and tidy. The furniture looked modern and clean. I didn't know what his role was in the disappearance of the two women, so I thought it was best if we stayed outside. It would be easy for him to overpower me and grab my gun. I could fight him, but I wasn't sure how well a fighter he was and would rather not take a chance.

"No," I said nonchalantly. "I shouldn't be long. We can stay out here, if you don't mind." I motioned for the chairs on his porch.

Todd sat in the loveseat while I sat in the single chair.

"Do you know Bianca Edwards?"

Todd eyes widened, pupils dilated. "Do you know where she is? I've been calling her cell, but it keeps going to voicemail."

"When was the last time you saw her?" I had my note-book in my hand.

Todd sat back with pain etched on his face. "About a week ago when we had dinner. It didn't go too well though."

That must've been the evening he had commented on her page and then disappeared from social media. "Tell me about that evening."

"We had dinner. We fought about the friend she was spending too much time with. And not enough time with me. I was jealous of her friend. I know, it's stupid. We spoke on Sunday though. She wanted to meet up today, but I haven't heard from her." He frowned again. "Why is a PI looking into her anyway?"

"Her dad hired us. Did you know about the procedure they booked her for on Monday?"

"Yeah, she told me about it. Her dad was taking her. That's why we planned to meet today. But I've been trying to get hold of her since yesterday to hear how her shoulder is."

I nodded as I made notes. "Do you remember a Rose-mary Haynes?"

He paled and stopped breathing for a moment. He exhaled audibly then blinked. "What does Rosemary have to do with Bianca?"

"You tell me, Todd. You knew them both." His demeanor hadn't changed apart from being shocked that I had mentioned Rosemary's name. "Why don't you tell me a little bit about her? How you met? And what happened to her?"

"She disappeared on me. They booked her for a proce-dure—" He slapped his hand over his mouth; I assumed it was because he had now realized how strikingly similar the cases were. He shook his head. "It's not me, if that's what you were thinking. I could never—" He choked on the words and wiped misty eyes. "I love both of them. Ask Mrs. Haynes, she understood what Rosemary meant to me." He shrugged. "I didn't know Bianca's dad all that well, but they were close. She didn't want to introduce me to her dad just yet, because our relationship was still new." He leaned back in the lover's chair and continued rubbing Felix's coat, deep in thought.

"I understand this is difficult for you to comprehend, Todd, but you seem to be the link between these two cases. And apart from the procedures they both had, can you tell me anything else?"

His large eyes glistened. "They both have beautiful strawberry-blond hair."

Chapter Twelve

I MET Ned at a diner near his house; he was embarrassed that it was untidy. The coffee was great, and I ordered dinner while I waited for him—steak and eggs. When the waitress brought my food, Ned arrived and ordered coffee for himself; he said he hadn't been hungry much the last couple of days but would try a salad bowl.

Ned sat across from me, his eyes swollen and red-rimmed. He was paler than yesterday, and his hair was scruffy.

"How are you coping?"

His shoulders sagged farther. "I don't know. I feel numb." He glanced up at me, his mouth in a tight line, his eyes seeing past me, like he was in a different world.

"Did Bianca ever mention a boy named Todd?"

"No." The lines between his eyes deepened. "Who's he?"

"It appears they were dating."

Ned's cheeks reddened. "She never mentioned him to me. Were they serious?"

"They were a new couple. I suspected she wanted to first wait and see how things progressed between them before introducing him to you."

Ned squared his shoulders and sat back. Some color returned to his face, and his eyes focused. He may have been feeling numb earlier, but he was feeling everything now. "Does he know where she is?"

"No. They planned to meet up today, but he couldn't reach her." I finished eating and sipped from my mug. "I told him what had happened, and it shocked him." I didn't know whether it involved him, but the coincidences between the two cases was too much to ignore. People could act, and I wasn't sure whether Todd was acting or if he was genuinely concerned —and that it happened to two of his girlfriends was suspicious. I also didn't want to tell Ned that Todd may be involved in a similar case; he might do something stupid. I didn't want to tell Ned about the other case at all. It might add fuel to his fire, and he could burn down the police station for not doing their jobs as effectively they should have. Or Ned could go on a rampage fueled with anger until we found Bianca. Both men were unknown to me, and I had to tread lightly with them.

I centered the rest of my conversation around Ned and how he was coping, which was not at all. Although he still visited the various construction sites where his men worked, he left it to his foreman to sort out the nitty gritty.

Once he grew quiet, I had my own agenda I needed to discuss with him. I sucked up the courage and dug in my heels. "Ned, can we discuss the deposit for my services, along with the daily rate?" I pulled a few bills from my wallet to pay for the food.

"Yes." He retrieved his checkbook, wrote the amount, signed it and handed it over. "What's next?"

"Thank you." I tucked the check into my wallet. "I want to look into a few leads—"

"What leads? Can I help?"

I shook my head. "Rather not, Ned. I understand you feel helpless, and I can appreciate that you want to help search for your daughter, but I think it's best if you leave it to me. I'll be in contact with the police, because it's still an open investigation, and, if I find anything, I'll need their assistance. And I'll either send you a message or call you every day to give you an update. So, go to work, and try to stay busy. It will help."

He rose from the booth, nodded and, deep in thought, said, "I will try." He glanced at me, eyes bloodshot. "Do you think she's still alive?"

I hated responding to this question. There was a fifty-fifty chance she was dead or alive. And I did my best to answer Ned as delicately as possible. "I don't know, but I will do everything I can to find her. I'm working with the police, and I won't stop until we know more." I squeezed his shoulder.

He thanked me for dinner, turned and left the diner while I paid.

On my way home, I called Marc to update him on my case.

"Todd seems very suspicious," Marc said. "Those coincidences are too great to ignore."

"I agree."

"What does Donnie think?"

"He didn't want me to speak with Todd, but I was in the area already. I'll give him an update when I'm done speaking with you."

"Okay. Let me know if you need anything."

"Yeah, will do." I turned onto my street. "I'm at home. See you in the morning."

"Dana?"

"Yeah?" I parked my car and sat for a moment. The silence of the night was refreshing.

"When were you going to tell me about the break-in at your house last night?"

I groaned inwardly. "I didn't want you to worry, Marc. And I'm going to kill Donnie."

Marc chuckled. "Call me if you need anything. You know my door is always open."

"I will. Thanks. Kisses to the kids."

He ended the call.

Donnie's phone went straight to voicemail. I messaged him to call me when he could; I needed to update him and needed more information on Todd. I grabbed my bag and notebook and climbed out of my car, locked it and went inside my house.

Nothing felt better than returning home from a long day to a quiet house. Once inside, I locked the door, set my bag on the counter, placed my Glock on the table and grabbed a beer. I walked through the house as I sipped the cold beverage, ensuring everything was clean after the tech team had dusted for fingerprints and all the windows were still closed. When I was satisfied I was safe, I relaxed. Pulling my laptop out my bag, I propped my feet on the coffee table. Even though Donnie was on Bianca's case, I still wanted to do my own digging. After a few swigs of beer, I started my search.

Billie, our tech master who assisted us with in-depth searches, had loaded a program onto my laptop where I could perform high-level searches without breaching any major agencies. To put it in layman's terms, I skated just above the surface for info without it being illegal. It was a search engine that looked a little deeper; it's how I got the doctor's home address, yet strangely, his cell number was nowhere to be found. I admitted I didn't use this search engine often, as it freaked me out. It made me feel guilty and dirty, like I was in the dark web, trying to buy something illegal.

A speeding vehicle had t-boned Todd's parents' car in an intersection. Both his parents had died on impact, including the other driver. It was only an accident, no foul play suspected. Todd had been a teenager, and they had left him everything—the printing company, their savings, home, and trust funds. Todd was wealthy. From what I remembered of his seemingly average house, the furniture looked expensive and most likely had been ordered from a catalog. It was neat and tidy, so he had to have someone clean for him; I doubted he did his own dirty laundry.

Todd's website for the printing company was modern, and it boasted multiple contracts from top-performing companies which he listed as regular clients. Said clients had written rave reviews about how the company had flourished under his management style. The actual printers were kept in a warehouse downtown in the industrial area. A video had been uploaded of the floor manager explaining what transpired daily. But no pictures of Todd existed anywhere. Apart from that one picture he was in with Bianca, there was absolutely nothing else. I added notes to my current list of comments in my notebook, finished my beer and set the laptop on the table to discard the bottle and fetched another cold one.

Now that I had more time and was not dead-tired, I continued my search. The complaints the patients had lodged against the doctor—the elusive Dr. Eltringham—were searchable, and, as Donnie had informed me, they had dropped them all. He had been a doctor for twenty-two years. It was almost as many years as he had been married. The nurse he had fallen in love with was his first theatre nurse. The website I found listed the medical center they opened together where they serviced low-income patients at a fraction of the cost. It gave a short history about them with a cute picture of the couple wearing scrubs.

To disguise evil tendencies as helping those in need, then this doctor fit the profile. He had the opportunity to take women either before or after the so-called *procedure*. The patients conveniently didn't have any records anywhere; therefore, if anyone came looking for them, the admission staff wouldn't know anything about them. Dr. Eltringham drugged them then wheeled them out the back —perhaps the same exit I had used yesterday. The patients would be incapacitated and could be taken against their will with no fight in them. The patients would be there on their own freewill and would allow the doctor to inject them with anything, because they trusted him. And he would use that trust against them. It would be so easy for him to advise his patients he wanted to give them something to calm their nerves when, instead, he knocked them out and abducted them. When they awoke, would they have had the operation, or did he perform other rituals on them?

I shuddered at the thought.

As patients, we trusted doctors and believed they were doing their best to look after us. But, when a doctor had certain cravings and needs, he had medicine at his fingertips and scalpels in his delicate hands.

If it was the doctor abducting women with strawberry-blond hair, then his wife had to have known. They lived together, worked together, and I was sure they *played* together. There were couples who killed together, and perhaps they were one of them. But then how did Todd fit into the picture—if at all? He had known both women, dated them even. But then what?

As I studied the picture of the couple in their scrubs, my mind raced. First impressions in my world meant everything. What did I feel when I saw them? How did they look? What was I thinking when I saw them? I had an advantage; I'd seen many faces of evil, and, even though their actions would say one thing, what I felt said something different—and I always trusted my gut feelings.

Mrs. Eltringham, the nurse, her blond hair wound in a tight bun on top of her head. She didn't need Botox, just a very good elastic to pull her hair back tightly on her head and out of her face; it lifted her smile automatically. She was curvy in all the right places and a head shorter than her doctor-husband. She had her arms around his waist with a playful smile plastered across her face; she was ecstatic to be there.

Dr. Eltringham, the doctor. His dark, almost black hair was cut short and neat out of his face. Brown hooded eyes pierced the camera lens, and it felt like he was staring right at me. It was eerie yet effective. They were the poster couple, an image of happiness and bliss—perfect for your Christmas stocking. He draped his arms around his wife's shoulders like she was his everything.

As I surveyed the happy couple, my thoughts conjured all the pictures I'd seen of perpetrators throughout my working career. The pictures for each assailant showed happy family portraits before they had supposedly performed an illegal act—smiling faces with not a care in the world. Yet, deep down, evil had manifested within each of them. What I'd realized then was that looks were deceiving.

Staring at the happily married doctor and his nurse suggested the same; all was not right.

Chapter Thirteen

ROSEMARY WOKE WITH A START. She pulled her arms, but they had tied her down. She was flat on her back, her arms and legs spread-eagle. She squeezed her eyes shut to remember how she got here, but she couldn't. The last thing she remembered was watching television. Unable to move, she wasn't sure what they would do to her. She'd never been here before, only her *room*.

A gentle breeze caressed her skin, and she now realized she was naked. Glancing down the line of her body, she saw the same masked figure in dark clothing; he was washing her feet. She twisted in her binds, but they were too tight to escape.

"You're awake." His words sounded muffled behind the kabuki mask, but she could understand him. Today, he looked like a devil; the kabuki mask was shaped like a laughing devil and painted black and red.

Rosemary whimpered, trying to pull free from his grip.

He edged near, a hand never leaving her skin. "Are you comfortable, my dear?" He touched her knee.

She shook her head, not wanting to speak, for fear her voice might fail her.

"I only want to bathe you. I need you clean." His hand caressed a hip bone. His index and middle finger walked up her stomach, ribs, breast and settled around her neck. He squeezed gently. "How does that feel?"

"I've been good. I haven't tried to escape again. Please let me go. I don't know what you look like, and I won't say a thing." Her vision blurred at the sides as he severed her airflow.

When he released, she coughed and inhaled deeply. He closed the gap between them, and she could see the detail of the black and red devil mask.

Her chest heaved as her heart pounded against her ribs, and the rush of adrenaline sent the drugs coursing through her veins quicker. Her sight shimmered, and now two masks were swirling into one another.

"You will be free soon. I need to make space for my new lovely. And I think it's time she moves into your room," he whispered, stepped back and tinkered with the drip. "Close your eyes and think happy thoughts." His voice sounded dreamlike.

Rosemary's vision tunneled as the black and red mask taunted her. As much as she struggled, she knew she couldn't stay awake. And, for once, she welcomed the drugs if it meant escaping from him. She relaxed and allowed the drugs to take effect.

Chapter Fourteen

I TRIED TURNING over onto my side, but something was stopping me from doing that and from getting comfortable. I had to get a new bed because this one was killing my joints. I slowly opened my eyes and stared at the ceiling. Moaning, I lifted my head slower; any sudden movement would send a cascade of pain throughout my body. Every single joint ached and was stiff. I'd fallen asleep in my armchair with my laptop still on my lap. I moaned again as I lifted the laptop and placed it on the table beside me. I moved one leg at a time off the coffee table then wiggled toes to ensure blood had properly circulated.

Only the light from the kitchen was on, and the light from the silver moon outside shone through the open curtains and splashed a mercury glow onto the living room floor. Placing both hands on the armrest, I pushed myself up. Once I was standing, I counted to ten, wiggled my toes again and rolled my shoulders. A crackling sound came from my neck as I moved it in circles. I groaned at the sudden jolt of pain, but it passed quickly. A slow walk to the spare bathroom was enough to oil my joints. Once done, the clock on the bathroom wall read 4 a.m. Since I was already up, I might as well shower and get ready for the day; I had lots to do.

After washing my body, I turned the hot tap full blast for a second before switching it off. The silence of the early morning was thunderous in my ears once the water was off; only drops of water from the shower head broke the silence.

Bang. Bang. Bang.

I stopped drying to listen. It sounded like an open window hitting the frame. Opening the bathroom door, I checked the dark hallway and the bedrooms I could see from where I stood and listened again. The banging sound continued as a gust of wind blew from my bedroom. I ran to the living room and grabbed the Glock off the table. The two spare bedrooms were clear. I waited outside my bedroom. *Bang*—the window hit the sill again. I pointed my gun in the window's direction as I entered my bedroom as the other hand kept the towel in place. The curtains moved inward from the wind, and the window opened again. I pushed aside the curtain, closed and locked it.

I dressed quickly and checked each room again. All the windows had been closed when I got home last night. Someone had opened my window. *Again*. I swore under my breath as the hairs at the back of my neck stood on end. Something didn't feel right. I suspected they were still around; my gut was telling me to look outside, even though it was a bad idea. I needed to see if they were still here.

Holstering the Glock, I went out back through the kitchen. Fresh, cool air greeted me; the moon's mercury shine illuminated the back yard. Crunching leaves alerted me to the right. I followed the sound around the corner of my house and to the side. The side gate swung open. The fence screeched. I moved through the gate. Movement caught my eye as the silhouette maneuvered behind the tree in my neighbor's yard. I jumped the fence and ran after them.

The figure bolted.

"Stop!" I yelled a few times while running.

The person was faster than me.

Lights came on at a house across the road. They were no doubt calling the cops; this was a *safe* neighborhood. If anyone was yelling this early in the morning, it meant it was an emergency.

We were heading toward the park. Swings moved as the figure ran between the two then behind a building.

I followed. As I turned the corner, an arm came for my face. I was lucky to see the arm before it hit me. As I fell to the ground, I swung my arm and connected between his legs.

He doubled over. His dark masked face was near mine, and I punched him again. He recovered quickly and hit me in the jaw.

Sparkly stars blurred my vision. I clenched my teeth upon impact and bit my cheek and tongue. The crunching sound in my jaw sent a sharp pain throughout. While still on my haunches with both hands nursing my jaw, the guy stood and ran. Wiping my eyes dry, I spat blood onto the grass beside me and rose to my feet.

Lights blinded me before I could take after him.

———

PRESSING the ice pack against my jaw was soothing, and my mouth had stopped bleeding. I pulled the blanket tighter around my body as I watched Donnie and James approach.

"You okay?" Donnie asked and sat beside me. "Could you see his face?"

"He wore a black mask. Even if he didn't, I couldn't get details. He was so close he was blurry. That was just before I saw stars." I lifted my hand holding the ice pack for emphasis.

"Do you think it's Pig-head?" James asked as he stepped closer.

"Don't know, probably, maybe." I shook my head. The weight of disappointment was overwhelming. "I was so close, he was right there, and I could've … but I didn't." I panned from James to Donnie. "I mean, if I wasn't so slow, but he was quick. He waited for me to chase him. You know what I mean?" I sounded incoherent. "Sorry, I didn't sleep well." I rubbed my eyes with my free hand.

Donnie put his arm around me. "It's okay." He hugged quickly then let go. "Before you say anything, you're staying by me, or I'm staying by you until we catch this guy."

Shaking my head made me dizzy. I swallowed hard to avoid vomiting and paused for a moment. "No, Donnie. Thank you, but no thank you. You have a wife and children to look after. I won't risk your or their lives."

"I'll stay with you. I don't have either. I'll be at your place around eight with my sleeping bag," James said with a grin.

"Thanks, James." Donnie stood and shook his partner's hand.

I leered up at him. "I can't let you do that either, James."

"I don't care what you want, Dana. If it's the same guy, he managed to come after you twice already. Suck it up, you need police help."

Chapter Fifteen

MARC WAS busy with the coffee machine by the time I pulled my ass into the office. Nigel was still out doing who knows what. My head throbbed, and I was fishing for painkillers out of my bag.

"You okay back there?"

"Yeah, I'll be fine," I grumbled. "Do you have painkillers? I can't seem to find mine."

"Here." Marc handed me the bottle. He stared at me with wide eyes. "What the hell happened to you?"

"You mean Donnie didn't give you the inside scoop yet?" I growled and rolled my eyes, which was a bad idea; sharp pain shot through my skull, and stars clouded my vision.

"Go home, Dana. You look like shit."

I gently rubbed my swollen cheek and jaw. The bruising hadn't started yet, but that would come. I'd bitten my tongue and the inside of my cheek, so my mouth was raw with a constant copper taste. And my neck hurt. It felt like I had whiplash, which I probably did. The perpetrator had hit me so hard and from the side that it snapped my neck in a sideways-backward motion. I'd been hit before, but never that hard.

I gently rubbed my neck. "Thanks, Dad, but I'm fine."

"I wasn't asking, Dana. Go." He scrutinized me from behind his desk. "Tell me what you need, and I'll do it. I just wrapped up my case load, so I have the capacity. My next client is only coming in next week." He rearranged pieces of paper and neatened his desk then steepled his meaty index fingers, his biceps straining against his green long-sleeve work shirt. His green eyes glistened in the florescent light. Marc wasn't angry often, but today he was for some reason.

I sighed, removed two tablets and swallowed them with yesterday's water. Marc's coffee was usually better than Nigel's, so I went to the kitchen for some. If it wasn't Donnie telling me what to do, it was Marc—and now James. Once my headache was gone, I would be fine and could continue with my current case.

I took my coffee into the open-plan office and stopped beside Marc's desk. "What's up with you today? Why are you so angry?"

Marc stopped writing, pushed his chair out and to the side, so he could face me. "Nothing, but I am worried about you. Have you seen your face?"

"I don't need to see it. I can feel it."

Marc disapprovingly shook his head. "Tell me," he commanded through a gentle whisper.

I gave him a quick rundown of what had happened.

Concern splashed on his face, then the red blotches started up his neck. "Okay, I've met James and glad he'll take the first shift tonight. I'll be over tomorrow night. I'll call Donnie later to discuss the details."

I gently shook my head. "Marc, no. I really wish you guys would stop doing this. It's not like I can't protect myself."

"Dana, it's not that. If this was happening to one of the guys, we would do the same. It's what we do. We don't know who this person is or from which direction he's coming from." He arched an eyebrow, and the red blotches spread across his entire face. "And, if there is more of us working together, the likelihood of us catching *him* is greater." Which made sense.

"Okay, fine," I grumbled. "But I'm not going home. If you want in on this case, we can work together."

"Great." He stood. "Now tell me what we're doing today."

Even though Donnie and James were busy with Bianca's case, so was I. I couldn't sit around and wait for something to happen. We were, after all, working together on this. We needed to know more about this doctor and his wife. We had all the information we could get from the resources we had, but I checked their website one last time. They had an online booking system for patient consultations. When I clicked on the blocks, it asked important information: name, surname, phone number, with a free text box where patients could leave the reason for the visit. And it gave me an idea. Not sure why I'd missed it last night. I must've fallen asleep while I was still busy. I had tried calling their medical center on my way to work this morning, but they were still closed. We needed proof they had seen Bianca, and one credit card receipt wasn't enough. And one way to access their information was via their own system. We couldn't ask Donnie for this, because he had to go the legal way, which could take a few days—which we didn't have. While we could still use *other* resources instead, and I shared my thoughts with Marc.

"Let's go see a man about a horse," he said.

I was still nursing my headache, so Marc drove. I reclined the seat and slept for what felt like five minutes, waking when we slowed at Billie's gate.

Marc pressed the button for the intercom. "Billie, it's us. Open up."

"Who's that with you?"

"It's just Dana. She's had better days."

The buzzer sounded, and the large iron gates opened. Once they were fully open, Marc drove up the long winding driveway and parked in the visitors parking. The mansion before us was at least a hundred years old. Billie came from old money and used his time wisely.

Billie waited for us at the front door, gave us cuddly bear hugs and offered drinks.

With our bottles of water, we followed him to his command center in the basement that also doubled as his apocalypse bunker. He watched too much news and was as paranoid as they came. I suspected he had other DSM-5 conditions, but would never, ever mention the topic. He was a good guy and always helped us out.

"To what do I owe the pleasure, Marc? You and Dana haven't visited me in ages. This one has to be good." Billie rubbed his bald head and massaged his thick neck.

"We've gone to the police and have information, but we need more. We know of two missing girls so far, but we need proof they were actually at the medical center, and we want to know if more women are missing." Marc sat on one of the visitor La-Z-Boy chairs.

I sat in the other; my body melted into it.

"Okay, what's the doctor's name?"

"Dr. Eltringham. I want a list of his patients and similarities between the patients. I want to know the types of procedures he performs. He may be a specialist in one procedure, then that's fine. But, if he consults on multiple conditions but only has one type of procedure that he performs, I want to see that too." I opened the bottle and drank some water. "I also want to know how these patients came to him. Were they in accidents, sports injuries—that type of thing."

Billie nodded as he wrote on a notepad.

"I also want to see if he has a *type*."

Billie whipped his head upward and eyed me, frowning. "What type of doctor is he, Dana? Please don't tell me it's a pediatrician."

"Orthopedic." I gave him the doctor's website.

"Okay, good." He made notes then typed on one of his curved keyboards.

Eight screens were stuck on the wall with four keyboards and four super computers. Billie used to work for the government, for various secret organizations where he would help them hack into computers that belonged to the bad guys they were tracking. He also worked on a super program that helped him find criminals who were on social media via facial recognition then track that person's where-abouts and whether they travelled across continents or not. This super program could track anyone using electronics, which was a scary thought. That's why I had to live in the apartment and house using my aunt's name and not mine. I had to be seen as invisible to Pig-head, so he could never find me. But, somehow, he had.

Billie had been good at his job until he stumbled upon a website in the dark web that had sent him crashing and hospitalized for anxiety and stress. He, much like me, quit after that and started his own business. He worked mostly on government contracts he wanted to work on and rejected those he didn't. And he helped us out when we needed him.

While Billie performed his ritualistic magic on his hardware, Marc went through Billie's things. Marc was a natural-born detective and used to work in the same department as Donnie, so the need to peek at everything was still in him. He lifted parcels, glanced at invoices, read notes. Billie was so busy with his computer and screens he didn't realize what Marc was doing and didn't chastise him like he usually did.

I grinned from ear to ear just thinking about how insufferable Marc could be sometimes and was glad I worked with him. When he had lost Rachael, he had to care for their daughter June—or Junebug—which wasn't easy. A hard-ass like Marc had suffered in the beginning, but he managed, and Junebug had blossomed into a wonderful eighteen-year-old. She was in Europe with friends and studying art. His two other *kids* were his Boston terriers, Chivas and Regal, named after his favorite whiskey.

I flinched when Billie hit keys and yelled, "Booyah! Okay, I got the motherfucker."

My heart thundered in my chest as my legs dropped to the floor. Marc was sitting beside me, and I couldn't recall him sitting down. I must've been more tired than I had thought.

"What, Billie? You're killing us with all the suspense," Marc demanded, growing impatient.

"Okay, okay," he said excitedly. "Dr. Eltringham has practiced for twenty-two years. He and his naughty night nurse started dating soon after he started operating. They married and had one daughter."

That was news to me. I'd never heard of them having any children. "How old is she?"

"Was. She died two years ago."

My arms pebbled. "What happened?"

"Doesn't say." He pressed keys and shook his head. "Nah, it's under lock and key. It'll take me some time, but I can find it."

"What else do you have for us?" Marc stood and placed his hands on the chair back.

"They have the worst security on their website, so it was easy for me to get the list of all their patients since they opened the medical center. That should help you in narrowing down the patients he sees. I've also sent you information regarding their financials and other info." He turned in his chair. "I think that's it, but let me know if you need anything else."

"Can you also check to see if his patients went to any other doctor after they saw Dr. Eltringham?" I asked and stood beside Marc.

"Sure. I'll crosscheck and send you that list once done. That part might take longer, because I'll need to do individual searches on each patient and where they went, but you'll get it tonight or early tomorrow morning."

I checked my cellphone; it was already late afternoon. I couldn't believe we had been here for so long. I must've fallen asleep for a few hours and not minutes, like it had felt.

"Thanks, Billie." Marc slapped his back. "Send us the bill." He chuckled and walked toward the hallway.

"As if I ever charge you." Billie rose from his seat, and I followed.

Chapter Sixteen

MARC STOPPED at a drive-thru for burgers and fries then parked at Navy Pier. It was completely out of our way, but he wanted to sit on a bench and watch the water while we ate. The breeze had a bite to it and the air moist. Although it was relaxing to sit here, my head started burning up, so I drank another painkiller. I picked at the fries—my mouth still hurt—had one more bite of the burger and set the rest on the bench between us.

"Not hungry?" Marc asked between mouthfuls.

"Nah-huh." I wiped my hands on a napkin. "You can finish it, if you'd like."

"Finish the fries, Dana. You hardly ate anything all day."

"Yes, Dad." I grabbed the basket of fries and ate slowly.

We watched the birds fly above us, heard the water lapping against the sides of the pier and listened to the music playing softly in the background. Passersby ate their fast food, carried sleepy children, laughed with friends, or watched the water, like we were.

"I haven't been here in years. What made you think to come here?"

"Rachel loved coming here." He glanced at me with misty eyes.

"I'm sorry." The memory of seeing her in the hospital bed with tubes and machines keeping her alive brought tears to my eyes, but I blinked them away.

"Don't be. What we shared was great, and I would never forget her. I enjoy coming here and remembering the fond memories of us." He finished my burger, threw away our trash and sat back down. "Sometimes you need to step away from the cases and smell the fresh air, Dana." He stared at me with one raised eyebrow. "You blink and your life is over and you're old with nothing to show for it."

I narrowed my eyes at him. "You sound like Donnie and my real dad when you get all philosophical and sentimental on me, Marc." I folded my arms.

"When this case is over, you are on leave for two weeks."

My mouth gaped open, and I scowled at him. "You can't do that."

"I don't care what you think, and I just did. You only take a day here or there, not even a full week at a time. I love working with you, but you need to take some time for yourself. I wanted to force you to take a vacation after the cheating husband case, but then this case came along. I'll help you on this one, and hopefully we can wrap it up sooner," he said, rising.

I still wanted to argue with him, but then he walked away from me. I ran to catch up with him, then a chill ran through me. I pulled my jacket tighter against my body as we walked to his car in silence.

The drive home was quiet, and, even though I still wanted to object to him telling me when I should take time off, I didn't. My head still felt warm and my body drained. That's when I knew he was right; I hadn't been taking proper care of myself.

Marc parked in my driveway, and I climbed out and walked to his side.

He opened the window.

"I'll go through the data Billie should've sent us already and will send you my findings. Read through it, then we can take it from there."

"Sure. Don't work on it too late. We can finish it tomorrow or Monday," he said as he reversed the car. He didn't give me a gap to protest as he waved and drove away.

I reached the front door as another car pulled up. Squinting, I saw it was James.

"Hey, did you just get home?" James yelled out his window.

I nodded.

"Where's your car?"

"At work. I'll get it tomorrow."

He climbed out, pulled a bag from his back seat and a rolled up sleeping bag.

"You really brought your sleeping bag." I pointed to the item tucked under his arm.

"I'll pretend we're camping." He grinned.

"Glamour-camping." I laughed and opened the front door. I froze in the doorway when I saw it. The red box. Red roses.

James moaned when he bumped into my back, our heads hitting.

I didn't feel any pain.

"What is it?" James pushed past me. "Motherfucker," he growled as he approached the large bouquet that sat on my kitchen table. Beside the vase was a red velvet box. "You definitely have a stalker." James removed the box's lid. His eyes bugged, then he quickly covered it again. Glancing at me, he shook his head once—a way of delicately telling me I shouldn't see what was inside the box. But James didn't know me all that well, and now I had to know what was in there.

"What's inside the box, James?" I moved toward him. His hands were still on the box by the time I reached for the lid, but he was keeping the lid firmly in place. "Let go, James."

He placed his hands over mine to stop me from opening the box. His hands were warm over mine. "Don't. It's gruesome."

"I gathered from the look on your face. Thanks for the warning, but I'm a big girl."

He released my hands, allowing me the choice to either open the box or not.

I lifted the lid wide enough, so I could see inside. I felt blood drain from my face and replaced with that icy feeling and cold sweat.

Chapter Seventeen

BY THE TIME Donnie and the other cops had left, it was almost 1 a.m. before anyone could move anything. The medical examiner had to confirm whether the heart in the box was human. Thank heavens it was only a pig's heart. But it was still disturbing. Maroon blood had soaked right through the velvet box and all over my kitchen counter. They had addressed the card in the bouquet of red roses to me, the words inked with pig blood.

Dana, watching you has been one of the most satisfying events in my life, and I hope to get reacquainted in the flesh soon.

SHUDDERING for the hundredth time just thinking about it, I realized it was something I'd have to discuss with my therapist. I'd been putting off our consultations for months; perhaps I should look into rescheduling.

I finished washing up in James's bathroom, switched off the light and climbed under the covers in one of his spare bedrooms. Lying in bed, my mind replayed the event over and over; me lifting the velvet box's lid and discovering the red organ—so red, so plump, so bloody.

After the grisly discovery, I had eventually agreed to stay at James's house but only for a short while. He had handed me a spare key to the front door, saying I was welcome to come and go as I pleased.

"James, I hardly know you," I had responded with a playful smirk. "It's too soon for us to move in together."

He had chuckled and had handed me a bath towel to use after my shower.

A smile splayed across my face as I imagined his laugh and kind honey-colored eyes. My eyes fluttered open. No! I would not go there. I immediately pushed any naughty thoughts about my brother's new-ish partner down and into a black hole. By trying not to think of him, that's all I did, wondering why he didn't have a wife or girlfriend to share his life with. I knew he had moved to Chicago from Vegas and, if I wasn't mistaken, had asked for the transfer.

My imagination ran away with me on the various reasons why he had relocated; his stripper girlfriend got into trouble with the mafia, his wife divorced him, the gambling bosses were after him, his old partner asked him to move. And so it went, my mind rambling on and on.

Lying on my back and staring at the dark shadows splashed across the ceiling, I thought of his kind words and how he had offered to help me. Beneath that hard exterior was a gentle soul, and I marveled that the job hadn't toughened him up or broken him. He had a luscious smile. I felt my lips curve upward. My eyes grew heavy, and I finally fell asleep and dreamt …

I PULLED *on my tight collar and loosened the top button of my blouse. It was hot inside the vehicle. The evening was upon us without a moon to light their way or to show me where they were. The car windows were tinted, so no one could see in, but I couldn't see out all that clearly either—especially on such a dark evening. Opening the window would be a bad idea. Alerting the fact someone was in the car would result in a bust and ruin our chances of an arrest. So, the windows stayed closed while I had to sweat it out.*

Movement near the column of the bridge caught my eye, and I sat forward, elbows propped on my knees with my chin in my palms. Squinting helped a bit, as I saw one person walk away from the column. I glanced at the shell of a long-ago burnt car where one of our men was hiding and watching, like the rest of us.

Another agent was behind the other cement column, and it amazed me they didn't use that one and find the agent. They probably would've killed him if they used that side, but it was more open and visible to passing cars. Instead, the assailant used the column that led to Bishop Ford Freeway; it was dark and somewhat hidden—the perfect escape.

Another agent hid in the gap between the column and the top of the bridge. Johnny was my direct report and a mountain climber over weekends, so it was second nature for him to scale the walls. The fourth agent was near me, near trash cans and under plastic; he was playing the stereotypical homeless vagrant, the FBI Special Agent hiding in plain sight.

I loosened the second button of my blouse and fanned my damp skin. It was exciting and scary at the same time. My first case, and I, Dana Mulder—no relation to any TV series superstar—had pinned down the location of the vigilante killers. It was actually four locations I had suspected, but they were at ours. I was glad we hadn't wasted resources by being here. That would've destroyed my career if no killer had appeared. But they did, and I was glad—career restored.

Another figure followed the first one.

"Stand by," the voice in my earpiece crackled, followed by white

noise. It sounded like my direct report, Johnny the mountain climber. But then again, he and another agent sounded very similar—that stoic stick-in-the-ass baritone that boomed, making me flinch in my seat. All four agents were scary yet fair.

Two more figures came from the dark shadows behind the column, and they carried something. I was literally on the edge of my seat as the crime unfolded, the proverbial body dump. I had initially said we were looking for at least two killers. Tonight revealed there were six of them —six killers who wore some type of mask to obscure their faces, with black clothing to complete their vigilante look. Wiping my palms on my tailored pants did not help; they remained damp no matter what I did.

The six dark shadows stopped directly under the bridge a short distance from the car I was in. All turned to stare in my direction. My heart stopped as I realized either they had seen me or suspected someone was in the car. But it didn't stop them. The two holding the body placed it on the ground and unwrapped it like one would a present on Christmas morning. A limp body rolled out. One of them folded the tarp or blanket—I couldn't tell from this distance—placed it in a back-pack and set it on the floor.

"Now," barked the voice into my ear again.

Yelling proceeded.

The six figures crouched and banded together in attack mode.

The four agents emerged from their hiding spots, weapons drawn and aimed at the six killers.

Johnny climbed down the concrete column and joined his team. That's when it all went to hell. One killer threw a knife before an agent could even think to pull the trigger. He cried in my earpiece with gargling sounds, like he was struggling to breathe through the blood, and crashed down. Silence echoed in my ears.

Two agents fired, but the killers were nimble, anticipating the shots, and maneuvered out of the way.

One killer jumped onto an agent and blasted out his brains, his face exploding and leaving a gaping hole in his head. It was so quick he didn't have a chance to make a sound. The killer rode his body until it hit the ground.

My earpiece was quiet. All I heard was my hammering heart. Cupping my hands over my mouth, I knew I needed to remain calm. The killers were slaughtering my fellow agents. I had to do something.

"I'm coming to help," I cried out into my mouthpiece to inform the remaining two agents. I knew I had to do something but couldn't remember what that was. All I could think to do was help them, and now.

"No! Stay!" Johnny barked.

I kept my hand on the door handle as I slowly and quietly opened it.

The other agent ran for one of the killers. He hadn't killed any agent yet, but he subdued the agent on the ground. They fought with fists and raw rage. The cries coming from that agent's beating was loud in my ear.

I ripped off the earpiece and threw it on the car's floorboard.

While they fought, four killers ran away as the two remaining vigilantes attacked Johnny.

I bolted out the car. The two killers turned to look at me as I ran toward them, my boots hard on the ground. Now that I could see them, I realized one killer wore the head of a bear.

He had beaten the other agent's face to a pulp; he lay motionless on the ground, his jaw slack and on his chest and in a bloody mess.

The pig-masked killer towered over Johnny who had a swollen face, and blood dribbled from his mouth.

"You should've stayed hidden," Johnny said through thick lips and a broken jaw.

As I neared, Bear-head caught me on my side, and I crumpled to the ground. Pain ebbed in my side as red liquid blossomed my white blouse. I leered at Bear-head, who was holding a sharp blade now dripping with my blood.

He wanted to attack again, but Pig-head blocked him with an arm and slowly shook his head. "Let me have her." He came closer.

I fell backward on my elbows, trying in vain to move away from him.

But Pig-head was quick. He was on top of me, straddling my waist as his meaty hands pinned my shoulders. "I agree with him." Pig-head tilted his head toward Johnny. "You should've stayed in the car." He leaned closer to my face.

I whimpered. The cold of the concrete burned my back, and I forgot about my wound.

"But I'm glad you came out to play. Now I can see what you look like up close." He pulled out a switchblade, flicked it open and ran it gently against my jawline. He did it again; this time, he applied pressure. Like a hot knife in butter, he carved into my soft, delicate flesh. The warm liquid ran down my neck. "Stay down if you want to live, or I'll see you again, sweetness, and I won't be as gentle as I am right now." Pig-head breathed near my ear.

I stifled my cries as I prayed.

He stood and motioned for Bear-head to follow him. "Come. There's nothing left for us to do here." He stared down at me.

"Are you crazy? You're leaving witnesses behind," Bear-head complained.

"Now!" Pig-head commanded then kicked Johnny in the ribs.

The distinct crack reverberated up my spine. I winced on Johnny's behalf, but he was out cold. I watched Pig-head and Bear-head leave the same way they had come.

Just before they disappeared into the darkness, Pig-head turned and stared at me for a heartbeat too long. The dark orbs where his eyes were penetrated mine for all eternity. He wanted me to remember him and to remember what he had done, the mark he had left on me for the rest of my life.

I JACKKNIFED OUT OF BED, my chest rising and falling as I struggled for air. I awoke in a cold sweat as my clothing and bed covers stuck to me. Frustrated and panicked, I kicked off everything when I untangled myself. I climbed out of bed, catching my breath and wondering where the hell I was. Once the disorientation had dissipated, the bloody red velvet box bore through my memories like a runaway train, and I remembered I was at James's house.

Once in the bathroom, I locked the door and splashed cold water on my face, hoping to rid myself of all memories —and of the night the vigilantes had attacked us and of the pig's heart in a velvet box. Surveying my face in the mirror, I noticed my skin was paler than usual with a bruise blossoming on my cheek bone from the assailant's punch to my face. Sometime between yesterday and now, I had also developed dark rings beneath my eyes. None of it was flattering. I lifted my shirt to see the knife wound to my side had healed easily leaving a faint scar. I raised my chin and ran an index finger along the scar; the thin raised pink tissue ran from under my left ear to the tip of my chin. The plastic surgeon had done a fantastic job, and the only way anyone could see it was if I lifted my chin or if someone shorter than me looked up at it. Otherwise, it was out of sight—but I knew it was there. Always. I recalled his stare as Pig-head had turned to look at me. He had imprinted that animal face into my memory, ensuring I never forgot him. And, with the physical scar, he had ensured I always remembered him each time I looked in the mirror.

Unwanted tears fell, and I couldn't stop them this time. I allowed myself to let go for the first time in a very long time. I knew I had to speak with Dr. Adams and soon. I couldn't continue like this.

I flinched at the soft knock on the door.

"Dana? Are you okay?" James's voice was soothing and calm from the other side of the door. It made me smile.

"I'm fine. Thanks, James." I splashed water on my face again, but my eyes were puffy and red. Fuck it. I couldn't do anything to hide this face, so I opened the door to see him standing against the wall in his boxers and a t-shirt, with a concerned expression.

"You sure?" He pushed away from the wall. "Why are your eyes so swollen?"

"It's nothing. Just a little nightmare, that's all," I said, entering the kitchen. "Hope you don't mind if I make myself some tea. Don't think I can go back to sleep just yet. You don't have to stay up."

"Sit down. Let me make it for you." He pointed to a chair, and I promptly sat on it.

"Thanks." I combed my hair with my fingers then rubbed my eyes; they were burning.

"Tell me about your dream."

I wondered whether I should. He was my brother's partner, and he already knew what had happened to me. But something seemed to stop me from opening up to people, to show them the real me, the raw emotional side I kept locked away. I hated rehashing what I had endured. I had enough nightmares to last me a lifetime. And I didn't need saving.

When I was quiet for too long, James approached and sat beside me, studying me. "What was your dream about?"

I didn't think James would stop asking me about it until I told him something. And it wasn't a session with Dr. Adams where I had to express my feelings in detail. It was just two people getting to know one another—I could do this.

"Every so often I dream about that night when three agents were murdered. How I tried to stop them from hurting my direct report, but they almost killed him. And, well …" I shrugged. "How I was injured." I traced my jawline with a finger.

James moved my hand out of the way and gently tilted my jaw upward, so he could see, and whistled. "Some scar you've got there."

His face was close to mine, and, for a second, we shared a comfortable moment. His index finger and thumb held my chin, his lips near mine as we stared at each other. The kettle whistled and switched off, breaking our shared connection. He grinned and removed his fingers from my jaw.

A chill ran through me. The heat coming off him had kept me warm. My cheeks flushed, and I groaned inwardly when I realized I had packed the oldest sleepwear from my dresser. The hole at the bottom of my shirt looked as if hungry moths had attacked it.

James made tea with honey. It was sweet, delicious, and calming.

"What make is this?" I asked, raising the cup to my lips again.

"Chamomile. Something my mother used to make for me when I had nightmares."

"Oh, how old were you?"

"Twenty-three."

"Did something happen?" I cringed when the words left my mouth. Of course, something had happened. Why would he have had nightmares otherwise?

He smiled as if he knew what I was thinking but didn't embarrass me further. "I'd just returned from serving two tours and after losing a friend over there. I came home from the mall one day and found my father hanging in the garage. He suffered from PTSD, and well,

I guess it was all too much for him, and he ended it that day."

My heart fell to the floor. I couldn't imagine what that must've felt like; my parents were still alive. To be so young and see so much pain along with a cruel world bent on war then having it all ripped to shreds by losing a parent must have been devastating. I placed my cup on the counter, stood and went to him. Not knowing what else to do so I did what I thought was best, I hugged him.

His body reacted like I had caught him slightly off guard, but he hugged me back.

He was warm against my body and smelled like soap with a hint of him beneath—musk. It sent my heart a flutter, and I let go, not wanting to linger and leaving either of us feeling uncomfortable. I sat back in my chair and drank more tea. Heat blossomed my neck and cheeks again.

"I'm sorry that happened to you," I blurted, drawing attention from the hug we had just shared.

"It was a long time ago." His cheeks were a healthy shade of pink.

"When last did you see your mother?"

"She died about four years ago from breast cancer."

Oh gods, I loved stepping in it. Next time I should get this type of information from Donnie first. "I'm so sorry. Didn't mean to dredge up such harsh emotions at this ungodly hour."

The clock on the wall read 3:38 a.m.

"It's okay. I don't mind telling you." He flashed a gentle smile, and warm, kind eyes stared back at me.

"And it is very early." I finished the tea and stood. "I should probably head to your bed ... I mean to the bed in your spare bedroom." I groaned silently. "You know, try to get a few more hours sleep before I head to the office in the morning." I rinsed the cup and set it upside down on the drying rack.

James chuckled behind me, which brought a smile to my face. As he rinsed his cup, our arms touched for the briefest moment.

Without looking at him, I mumbled an embarrassed goodnight and went to bed.

Chapter Eighteen

WAKING up with sunlight on my face sent goosebumps all over my body. Blinking rapidly, I didn't recognize the crisp white walls, art deco side tables, or the hanging lavish paintings. I spotted my suitcase then remembered what had happened last night and why I was here. The clock on my cellphone read 10 a.m. An icy feeling washed over me, and I flew out of bed. I was never this late for work.

Marc knew what had happened last night because Donnie had spoken with him. Those two were always speaking behind my back, and, for once, I was grateful and lay back down on the bed. I wasn't in a hurry. In fact, Marc had sent a message that I should work from home or here for the day, and he would see me on Monday.

As I lay on my back, clutching my cellphone to my chest, I breathed deeply. Feeling my forehead, I noticed I still felt a little warmer than usual. I decided I would start taking better care of myself—less intense workdays, more me-days.

Once dressed, I walked through James's large house. He

had left a note saying he was at work and that I should make myself at home.

The house was quiet, which was something I wasn't used to, along with the neighborhood. He stayed in the upper side, where large families lived, surrounded by more open space than I'd ever seen. His sprawling back yard met up with rows of trees, which made it seem like he owned a mansion in a forest. His neighbors were at least a mile away on either side, so he could throw a party, and no one would complain. The house boasted three large bedrooms, with the main bedroom the size of my living room and kitchen together.

I opened drawers and closets, only finding the usual clothing for men. Nothing seemed to scream psychopath, like a skin suit. James might be a detective, but some people still had fetishes no matter their occupation.

When I finished snooping in his bedroom, I went to view his back yard in all its splendor. I shed a tear as I absorbed the landscape, wishing my place was half as big. James had to have come from money; he could never afford all this on a detective salary.

A blue sparkly pool called out to me, and all I wanted to do was swim and lounge about. But it was chilly, and I had work to do. A missing girl was out there who needed our help, but that didn't mean I couldn't enjoy it all the same. Once I had my first cup of coffee, I sat on a deck chair. I tested the table and realized it was high enough for me to work from.

By 1 p.m. I had eaten and enjoyed two cups of coffee and finally fired up my laptop. Billie had sent me three emails with various attachments I would have to delete permanently everywhere once I was done with it. Accessing patient data was a HIPAA violation that could land me in serious hot water, and I thought it best not to let anyone know how I had managed to obtain it. I opened the first email that contained the spreadsheet listing all the patients Dr. Eltringham had seen since he opened his medical center. Remembering I'd asked Billie to send another spreadsheet, I closed that one and went to the last attachment. Here he had added the list of other doctors who had seen the same patients as Dr. Eltringham. I wanted to understand which patients saw other doctors after they had consulted with Dr. Eltringham; I wanted to know whether his skills as a doctor were questionable or if he was good at what he did.

After carefully reviewing the data with various pivots and tables, I surmised about eighty percent of his patients had undergone some type of shoulder procedure, which told me he specialized in shoulders only. Those patients he had treated prior to two years ago seemed fine. But patients he had treated from two years until now almost all had consulted with another orthopedic specialist soon after their procedure with Dr. Eltringham. This was shocking; had the death of his daughter been what had caused his decline or something else?

Reviewing the various graphs I had produced, I could understand why at least ten percent of his patients saw other doctors, especially if complications had arisen during a procedure or afterward with their post-op care. But ninety percent of the eighty percent of his patients who'd undergone procedures had seen another specialist, which was alarming. The other twenty percent were only consultations and only seen once. And this was for the last two years; the previous years, he hardly had any patients who saw other doctors for second opinions, which meant something serious had happened, and he had hurt patients.

Next, I filtered out those ten percent who didn't see another doctor. I wanted to understand why, since most of his patients had sought second opinions. I noted two of these patients were already missing—Rosemary and Bianca. It was also the proof he had consulted with them—two consultations each and their procedure, which they had claimed directly from their insurance.

Somehow Billie had managed to find the raw data within their database, and their names were still available. I suspected the nurse or the doctor who had deleted those patients from their system thought it was gone forever, but it wasn't.

This shifted my suspicions back on the doctor. They had denied seeing these patients, yet here they were. And that perhaps Todd knowing both was coincidental, or he was working with the doctor somehow.

The ten percent resulted in fifty patients; ten of them were old and had died. Thirteen had moved away, twenty were in retirement villages or living in nursing homes, and lastly, seven remained with blank spaces next to their names. It was unknown what had happened to them. I panned across the spreadsheet to view the data in the other columns and noticed all their consultations had happened in the last eighteen months. My arms pebbled. This was good news but also terrible news. And they were all women.

I sent Billie a message, asking him to give me detailed information on these seven women. I wanted to know their hair and eye color, where they stayed, and anything else he could get his hands on—I wanted it all.

I opened the last email, which had two attachments. The first attachment was the financials relating to the practice of the medical center and Dr. Eltringham's personal bank statements. The other attachment listed all his properties—the medical center, his personal home, two rentals for storage, and apartments in Orlando and San Francisco.

The garage door opened, and a car pulled in, then the door closed. A few seconds later, James entered his house. "How has your day been?"

Glancing over my shoulder, I watched him climb down the steps, pull out a chair and sit across from me. I knew he and Donnie worked cases together and most likely on the Bianca case. I wasn't sure how much I could tell him, especially since I had obtained information illegally. I would have to be careful.

"Productive. I've been looking into a few things, which has revealed a lot about how Dr. Eltringham is as a doctor."

"Donnie said you would call him if you found out anything." He smiled and sipped from his beer.

"I will."

"Or you could tell me …"

I smiled guiltily as the silence stretched between us. It wasn't uncomfortable, but it made me feel uneasy, like he was silently judging me.

"How was your day?" I asked, maintaining the conversation.

"No prints were lifted at your house other than yours and Donnie's. The gift in question is easily accessible. Unfortunately, we're back to square one with your admirer."

I cringed. "Please don't call him that. He's a murderer, and the only reason why I'm not dead is because of pure luck and that he is crazy." The pig's heart was a message from Pig-head, and I couldn't ignore it anymore—a message he had found me again, after all these years. He had returned to haunt me in real life and not only in my dreams.

James stared at me mid-sip, stunned by my comment.

I shrugged. "What? It's the truth. If this guy wasn't so fixated on me, I would've been dead four years ago. And now he's taunting me. Again." I reached for his beer bottle, which he handed to me. I took two huge gulps, finishing it. "Sorry, I was thirsty." I handed the empty bottle back to him. "Next week is the four year anniversary."

"Why didn't you tell me? That's important information we could've used long ago. It's more serious than I thought, and we need more guys on this."

I lifted my hand to stop him from dashing up to make a call. "I would've thought Donnie told you the date."

James shook his head.

"It doesn't matter. Pig-head is focused, and no matter who is on it or how many, I'm sure he'll find me." An uneasy feeling sat in my diaphragm, and I struggled to breathe. "I don't know what he has in store for me. Are you sure you still want to be near me when it happens?" I raised an eyebrow. "If we can't stop him, it could get you killed."

He stared at me for a heart beat. "You want a beer?" he asked, changing the subject.

I nodded.

He returned with two beers and handed me one. "Let me think what we can do, and I'll discuss it with Donnie. Is there anything else you can tell me in the meantime?"

"No, there's nothing else to say. You know all of it."

"You said they killed only three agents. What happened to the fourth?"

"He was my direct report—Johnny. He survived. He's wheelchair bound and suffered a stroke while in the OR and has been on medical leave since. We chat once a month, and, from what he's told me, he only consults now. There's no way he can return to work."

"Jesus!" James downed half his beer. "Okay ..." He exhaled. "Before we panic, we need dinner. Have you been to the restaurant on Summer Drive?"

I shook my head, taking a sip.

"I've heard it's great. Throw on something a little more formal." He eyed my shirt and sweats.

The lines between my eyes deepened, leering at James. "Can't we get takeout instead?"

"I prefer to enjoy my food slowly. I hate fast food. It gives me indigestion." He entered the house again. "Be quick. I want to leave in ten minutes," he yelled from the kitchen.

I closed my laptop, brought everything inside and dressed for the evening. I'd emptied everything from my bag onto the bed and stared at the items. I didn't bring any evening clothes, because an extravagant dinner was far from my mind. I dressed in my black work trousers and a lavender blouse and combed my fingers through my auburn hair. Luckily, I'd washed it last night and didn't need to do much now. My hair was manageable on a wash-and-go system. No straightening required.

A soft knock came on the door. "Are you ready?"

"Yeah, just give me a sec!" I yelled, pulling on my boots. This was the best I had; it's not like we were on a date. It was only dinner.

———

THE WAITER HELPED me into my seat, but because I'd kept my gun in the belt holster, I had to wear a jacket over, and I was getting hot. The restaurant was empty apart from us and another couple in a booth across the room. I removed the jacket before I spontaneously combusted.

The waiter glanced at my hip and quickly averted his eyes. "Some wine, sir?" He handed the drinks menu to James who perused the list.

He handed the drinks menu back to the waiter and ordered a wine I'd never heard of from a late harvest. Which made me curious, so, when the waiter left, I had to pepper him with questions.

"So ..." I started, waiting for him to look at me. "You know your wines?"

He smirked. "Don't you?"

"Not to that extent. You seem to know a lot more than whether it's dry or sweet."

His smile lit up his face, and his eyes brightened. "My mom was a connoisseur of fine living, and wine was part of her teachings."

I nodded in understanding. She sounded like a wonderful lady who did right by her son. "You intrigue me, Detective Michaels. Is there anything else you wish to shock me with today?"

James sat back in his chair and considered my question, folding his arms over his broad chest. His navy-colored suit was tailor made and fit his toned body perfectly, accentuating the finer lines. I licked my lips and noticed he had seen. I mentally high-fived myself. Somehow, I still had it in me to attract the opposite sex—even though it never lasted longer than a few months.

"I've only had one serious girlfriend. When I asked her to marry me last year, she said yes. Only to sleep with her brother's friend ten days before our wedding."

I abruptly closed my mouth and kept quiet. It seemed like he had more he wanted to share, and I didn't want to interrupt him.

"That was the best day of my life, because I'd rather

find out before than live with someone for years and then find out." He leaned forward with his elbows on the table, his clothing taking strain against powerful arms. "That same day, they offered me a lucrative position to come here, which I didn't hesitate to take. I'm thrilled I moved here, because I met someone who I want to get to know on a personal level, and I hope she allows me." His gaze was penetrating, and I fought not to look away.

What he said suggested he was talking about me, but I wasn't sure. I never assumed. I preferred facts, but it didn't sit right to just ask.

"Your turn, Miss Mulder. What is it you are looking for?"

I swallowed hard, unsure what to say.

The waiter saved me when he delivered the bottle of wine. He offered a taste to James, who swirled the ruby liquid in his glass, sipped then nodded. The waiter poured wine in my glass first then topped off James's.

"You were saying ..." he said, interrupting my thoughts.

I followed his lead and sipped the red wine. It was an explosion of flavor bursting in my mouth, with a hint of fruit and nuts and a touch of vanilla, and it was neither dry nor sweet. It was frustratingly perfect.

"This is a great wine," I said and took another sip. "Right. What am I looking for? That was your question?"

He nodded.

"To be honest, I don't know, James. I work. I help those lost and try to get them back on track. That's what I do." I recalled Marc's discussion about me having to take more time for myself. "I'll admit, I haven't been great at taking care of myself, and, when I'm done with my current case, I'm taking a week or two off. Not sure what I'll do, but I'll figure it out when the time comes."

The silence between us was comfortable, and I felt at ease in his company.

He downed the rest of his wine and poured himself more. We ordered our meals, and the conversation flowed as smoothly as the fine wine we were drinking. We ate, we laughed, and we enjoyed each other's company. We only spoke of ourselves and not the case, which was a breath of fresh air.

Every so often, I had to move my gun and holster, so it didn't dig into my ribs, but other than that discomfort, I forgot about everything except for the man in front of me and enjoyed myself.

Chapter Nineteen

THE NEXT MORNING, I woke with a terrible headache and was grateful it was Saturday morning. Groaning, I climbed out of bed without my head exploding. The smell of coffee brought me to the kitchen where James was pouring me a mug.

"How are you feeling?" he asked with a playful smirk.

"I can't remember the last time I drank so much wine." My headache disappeared once I had coffee in me, and it was great coffee. I sat at the kitchen island, wrapping my hands around the warm mug. Outside, the rain lashed against the window as the wind blustered. The ground was already underwater, and the skies were dark grey with no sign of waning any time soon.

He chuckled, knowing it was his fault I had drunk wine. "But you enjoyed yourself though?"

I nodded.

"Good. What are we doing today?"

I raised an eyebrow. "We?"

"Yes." A smile splashed across his face. "You agreed we would do something today."

"I can't. I have a case that needs investigating." Which reminded me, I grabbed my laptop from the coffee table, placed it in front of me on the kitchen island and fired it up.

"We can do something this morning, and then you can continue with your case this afternoon." He pulled out a chair to sit beside me. "I can even accompany you, if you'd like."

"Are you one of those guys who has weekends to himself? And thanks, that would be nice." Donnie never accompanied me on any of my investigations. With James tagging along, perhaps I could learn a thing or two about how he did things, even though I was sure I was doing fine. I frowned at my laptop. It was taking forever to switch on.

"We're always on duty and go where the evidence takes us. But, if you don't take time for yourself, you burn out. And the cases aren't going anywhere, Dana. By Monday, there will just be more. And there's always more. So I take one day at a time. But, for you, I will make an exception and ride with you. A day in the life of Dana Mulder." He winked. "You know, Donnie does the same thing."

I arched an eyebrow.

"I promise. I've been here five months, and he tries to spend a Saturday morning or afternoon home. Those few hours are precious to his family."

I knew Donnie took time for Sunday lunch, but I was a little shocked to learn he gave his family a couple hours over a weekend. My heart burst with pride at the revelation. It also made me sad, guilt rearing its ugly head. I worked every weekend—all weekend. The only time I had for myself was a few hours when I had lunch at my parents' house on Sundays. Perhaps I needed to do the same, but it was just easier for me to work.

"Technically, we're both working the same case. At least give me the morning?" he asked.

As I stared out the window, I didn't think we could do anything. Once the laptop sprung to life, I saw there weren't any emails from Billie anyway. I had the names of the seven women who may or may not be missing, but, without addresses or any other information, I was stuck. I had to wait for Billie's input. If James and I worked together, perhaps he could fill in the missing info. If I told him what I knew, it may take time to get the information anyway, therefore I might as well do something with James this morning. I sighed, not wanting him to know I'd given in to his charm so easily.

"Okay, fine, but what can we do? It's raining." I jerked my chin toward the window.

"For one, I don't feel like making breakfast. How about we start there and see what we can come up with?"

BY THE TIME we finished breakfast at the diner, the rain had stopped. James made light conversation throughout the meal and peppered me with questions about Donnie and the other two detectives who worked in their unit.

"Lip isn't my favorite of the two, but Stuart always sizes me up like I'm meat. But then again, he does that with all women. If I can avoid them, I will. Donnie knows I hate interacting with them."

James nodded knowingly. "You aren't the first to raise those issues. The problem definitely lies with them. Have you ever considered filing a complaint?"

"You're joking, right? I could never do that. Everyone knows I'm Donnie's kid sister, and to complain about the people he works with will not go down well for him or me. Sometimes I need to come to them for help on cases I work. I won't be able to if I complain."

"You're right." James pulled money from his wallet and placed it on the table. "How about we go for a walk?"

We both stood, and he proffered an elbow for me to take.

"You're quite the gentleman, James. I don't think I've ever met any guy who still did this."

"Chivalry isn't dead, my dear." He winked.

We walked a couple of blocks until we came upon a park where kids were playing. As we reached the slide, my cellphone pinged. It was a message from Billie letting me know he had sent me information on the women I had asked for. I struggled to see emails on my phone, so I never bothered setting it up, and working with spreadsheets was better done on a laptop anyway. Not knowing what Billie meant, I needed to check my email as soon as possible. I felt guilty wanting to break our walk short, but I had work to do. And I didn't think James would mind, since we were both on the same case anyway. My laptop was still at James's house, and I was eager to see what Billie had sent me.

"We have to go," I said, apologizing with my eyes.

"Did you get the information you asked for?"

I nodded.

"I said I would join you, Dana," James said, smiling. "Where to first?" He turned around, so we could go back to his car.

"Well, I forgot my laptop at your house, so we need to go back and get it."

He nodded and offered a hand.

I hesitated at first but then took it.

He gently squeezed my hand, and we walked to his car in silence. His hand was warm around mine, causing my heart to flutter. James walked like we were just another couple going for a Saturday stroll, which left me smiling.

I should've been skeptical, said no and continued with the case on my own. But I was oddly comfortable and decided not to listen to my inner reservations and to just let it play out. Whatever it meant, to just let it be.

Once we were at his house, I read Billie's email and opened the spreadsheet. I scanned the data. The first name was Mildred Bordeaux, missing since 2013—the same year their daughter died. What made her stand out was she was the first one to go missing. The second person on the list went missing six months after Mildred had, and the third girl went missing only a month after the second. Billie had provided hair and eye color for the others but not Mildred. He was unable to obtain any pictures of her. All the women had strawberry-blond hair. There was something about the first person who had kickstarted this entire psychotic pattern and trail of events two years ago. Women were missing, and the police hadn't pieced it together. It was a blessing that James would accompany me, but it meant I had to tell him everything, all the info I'd dug up so far.

Then, in the email's body, Billie had given me two names of girls who were friends with Dr. Eltringham's daughter. I jotted down their addresses and turned toward James to tell him everything and where we had to go first.

Naturally, he wasn't happy I'd withheld information, but he understood why.

"I would never rat you out, but you can't withhold information again, especially if it's important to the case. You understand?"

I nodded.

"Just don't tell me who pulled the information for you."

"I won't, and thanks."

James took a moment to use his cellphone before we left. He wanted someone to do a similar search to what Billie had done. If anything happened, the investigation was still above board and legal.

———

KNOCKING on a maroon door with splintered wood made me cringe. It was like nails down a chalkboard. With each knock, the door rattled and grinded against the doorframe. The sound alone was enough to get all the hairs on the back of my neck to stand on end. I knocked one last time. Nobody answered.

"I don't think anyone's home," James said as he turned to walk down the stairs. Just as he reached his car, the door opened a crack.

"Yes?" a woman asked from behind the door. All I saw was her one blue eye swimming in darkness.

"Mrs. Bordeaux?" I leaned in so she could see me.

"Hmm."

"Can we come in and talk with you?" I added.

James walked back when he heard the door open.

"Why?" She closed the door slightly, not wanting strangers in her house.

"I'd like to talk with you about your daughter Mildred. I understand she's been missing for some time."

"She's dead," Mrs. Bordeaux snapped.

I had known she was missing, not that she was dead.

Billie hadn't found any other information on the seven women's whereabouts, so we had assumed they were missing.

"How do you know?" I asked, my tone soft and gentle. "I thought she was only missing."

"We found out she had died about six months after she went missing," she croaked, opening the door wider. A tiny woman looked up at us, panning from James then to me. "Why do you care about my daughter?"

"My name is Dana Mulder. I'm a private investigator and hired by a father looking for his daughter. I discovered other cases similar to his daughter's disappearance, and I was just following up on those leads. And one of those cases was Mildred Bordeaux who went missing about two years ago. I wanted to find out from either you or your husband what had happened."

Mrs. Bordeaux opened the door and waddled deeper inside. "Well, come in. I'll start the tea."

I stared at James, shrugged and entered.

Chapter Twenty

JAMES and I stood in the kitchen with Mrs. Bordeaux while she made us tea. She apologized for not having any coffee, but her doctor had said she couldn't drink any, so she didn't bother keeping any around. James offered to carry the tray to the living room, but she shooed him away, carrying the teapot, cup, and saucers herself, and placed them on the table. She sat on the chair closest to the table and poured tea into the cups.

While Mrs. Bordeaux was being the gracious host, James and I looked at the pictures on the walls of Mrs. Bordeaux with a man and a girl with raven hair like her father and blue eyes like her mother. Unfortunately, it didn't seem like Mildred fit our kidnapper's MO, who preferred strawberry-blond women. Mildred was as short as her mother, skinnier, natural black hair, and glacier eyes.

My shoulders sagged when I jerked my chin at the picture.

James nodded in understanding and sat down.

We were here, and Mrs. Bordeaux had already made us

tea. The least we could do was to speak with her even though it may be a dead end. I also didn't think she entertained guests often.

"Tell me ..." Mrs. Bordeaux poured milk into our cups. "What made you think my Mildred was still missing?"

"That was the information we had." I hoped I didn't come across as coldhearted as I felt. "We have a list of women who had gone missing the last two years, and we would like to find out if they relate to our current case."

"I see." Mrs. Bordeaux handed us a cup of tea, each with a home-baked cookie on the saucer. "My Mildred was found about six months after she went missing. Surely that information would be with the police. They were the ones who notified us."

I glanced at James, who was already typing on his cellphone.

"I'm an investigator, and sometimes information doesn't always find its way to me, so I need to go to the source. Apologies if this is bringing up any bad memories for you, Mrs. Bordeaux."

"Don't concern yourself, miss. I don't mind answering your questions."

I retrieved my notebook. "How old was she?"

James's cellphone pinged, and he read the message.

"Twenty-five."

"Is your husband still around?"

"Oh, no, poor soul. When the news of our baby girl came, he had a heart attack about a month after her funeral."

"I'm sorry." I cringed inwardly. "It's only you in this large house?" I scanned the vast living room; it would be a nightmare to clean, especially for just one person.

She smiled meekly and nodded. "Yes, it's only me."

"Do you know what had happened to your daughter?"

"Well, the police suspected she knew the person who had taken her. Either she went willingly with them at first or was kidnapped. We don't know for sure. A jogger in a park found her body six months later. After the autopsy, they said she had been alive for the six months and kept in good health but then killed for some or other reason."

"I'm sorry to ask this, but do you know how she died?"

Tears filled her eyes, and her chin trembled. After a moment, she finally answered, "They strangled her—" Those were the only words she could get out before she broke down.

My heart ached for her. I'd dredged up memories of her daughter's murder, and guilt tugged at my chest. She was a lonely, old woman with no one else in her life, apart from terrible memories of her only daughter and how they had killed her.

Dying by strangulation was classified as personal. Abusers in relationships used it as power to control the victim's next breath by using their bare hands, who they could kill within minutes.

"Did Mildred have a boyfriend?"

"Yes, but for the life of me, I can't remember his name. They weren't together long when she vanished."

The rest of the interview we made small talk. I didn't want to ask her any more questions about her daughter. It was painfully obvious we had opened old wounds and I hated myself for not knowing all the information beforehand. We finished our tea and cookie and left the poor woman.

Once we were in the car, James spoke for the first time since we had arrived at Mrs. Bordeaux's house. "I asked a uniform to send me information on this case as soon as he gets it." James reversed out the driveway and merged into traffic.

"And?" I asked, suddenly intrigued and hoping the officer had completed the request and had found information for us to use.

"This was Lip's case. He interviewed Mildred's boyfriend, but he had a watertight alibi, and there weren't any other leads. It was an open case for a while, and then it became a cold case. I've asked the officer to send me copies."

"Thanks, James. I appreciate you sharing it with me."

"No problem." He went quiet, his attention back on the road. After a few seconds, he added, "So, where to next?"

"Well, I was thinking about that. I don't feel like visiting another parent until we know the outcome of these missing girls. I don't want to upset another parent. It's awful what we did back there. How quickly can the officer send us the info? That way we'll know exactly where we stand instead of trying to work blindly." And that the police had sourced the list of women and was not an illegal search.

"A couple of hours to sift through the database. They're searching for all unsolved missing cases the last three years, narrowed down to women, then to strawberry blondes. Then we can compare it to your list. What else?"

"I was thinking of their daughter, that somehow Dr. Eltringham and his wife Mary might have lost the plot after their daughter died. Before we approach the doctor, I want to speak with her friends. Billie gave me two names I thought we could visit."

"Sure. Where to first?"

I found the whole situation of ours strange. He was a detective and taking orders from a female PI. I wanted to question his motives but then thought to rather leave it.

After our dinner last night, I suspected he liked me, and this was a way for him to spend time with me. He could get to know me a little better and solve the case, killing two birds with one stone. But I also knew men had egos and rarely took instructions from a woman, which James didn't seem to mind doing.

"You don't mind that I'm telling you where to go?" I asked nervously.

"No." He parked the car and gave me his attention. "Yes, this is an open investigation that Donnie and I are working. And PIs generally don't work with us, but there are exceptions, like now. If Lip and Stuart had their heads on right, they would have already done this. But they didn't, and we are. I want to find Bianca, and, if more women are missing, I want to solve this as much as you do. By teaming up, you can do your job, and I can do mine. And I don't see an issue with us doing it together. Unless you do?"

"No, I don't." I grinned as I gave him the address for one of Dr. Eltringham's daughter's friends.

James merged with traffic again. "What's their daughter's name?"

"Uh …" I scanned Billie's email again. He'd only mentioned her name once, and there were no pictures of her. No wonder I forgot. "Issy. Yes, Issy. Says here she had a heart attack. She was in her early twenties, died in hospital following a car accident."

"That's young."

While James drove to the address I'd given him, I reviewed the girls' info Billie had sent. The friends had lived on the same block since they were born. And the two girls we were going to see still lived at their parents' houses.

RASHIKA BROUGHT out a photo album to show us a few pictures of Issy and Felicity. Rashika Mansoor had olive skin, dark hair, and big eyes. Felicity was pale and blond with green eyes. Issy was sun kissed with freckles and long flowing strawberry-blond hair.

James and I shared a knowing look; Issy fit our kidnappers MO.

"Issy was in a car accident," Rashika said. "She'd broken bones and had internal injuries. When she had her fourth procedure in two weeks, her heart gave in. Her dad had said she might not have been coping well with so many procedures in such a short time. It was a shock to us. One moment, we were speaking to her; the next, she was gone." Rashika's eyes misted, and she grabbed a tissue.

"How long ago was this, Rashika?" James asked delicately.

"Two or three years ago." She frowned. "I think it was a little over two years, 'cause it was the same time as my brother's wedding."

"Thanks," I said, taking notes. "Is there anything else you can think of?"

"No."

"Did she have a boyfriend or date anyone casually? Anything like that?" James asked.

"No, not that we knew of. She focused more on her studies. She wanted to be a specialist, like her dad. Everything was about studying. We only saw her once a week. The rest of the time, she had her nose in her books." She closed the photo albums and packed them away. "She was closer to Felicity, so she might know something I don't."

"Before we go, did you know a Mildred Bordeaux?"

"No." Rashika quickly shook her head.

We thanked Rashika for her time and left.

FELICITY'S PARENTS' house was four doors down from Rashika's, and a grey-haired man wearing boxers and an inside-out dirty t-shirt answered the door. "Who are you?" the old man grumbled, eyes twitching with enlarged pupils.

"Is Felicity here?" James asked, stepping closer to the old man.

"Who?" he barked, raising a twitchy eyebrow.

"Dad, I thought I asked you not to answer the door," someone said from inside the house, followed by footsteps. The door opened to reveal a woman who resembled the picture we had just seen in Rashika's photo album. Felicity grabbed her dad's shoulders and pulled him away from the door. "Sorry about that. Come on in. I just want to take my dad to his room. Have a seat. I'll be with you in a second."

I closed the door behind me and followed James into the living room as Felicity walked her father down the long hallway. We scanned the room then walked alongside the wall where the photos hung. There were no pictures of a woman anywhere with Felicity, only a man who was a younger version of her dad. There were also pictures of the three friends in various stages of their lives, from their teens to young adult. The last picture on the wall had been taken at least four years ago, if I had to take the fashion into consideration.

"Can I help you?" Felicity stood in the doorway behind us with crossed arms.

"We'd like to speak with you about Issy."

"Rashika phoned me saying you might come by." She leered at us without moving from her spot. "Issy's dead. What more do you want to know?" Her tone was cold and unwelcoming. I wasn't sure if she had an issue with the police or if there was something else.

"I'm Detective James Michaels. This is Dana Mulder."

"Do private eyes and detectives always work together? I thought you hate each other."

Rashika must have also told her I was a PI.

"Not at all, but then again, I guess it all depends on the detective and the PI," James added nonchalantly.

"Issy was in a car accident and in the hospital for more than two weeks. During the fourth procedure, she didn't make it. They said it was a heart attack or something," she said, still not impressed with us. "Her funeral was beautiful. Her mom and dad went all out, and everyone who knew her was there."

"Did she have a boyfriend at the time?"

"No. Her studies came first, but …"

"What is it?" James asked, pressing her.

"Someone attacked her one evening when she came home from a study group session. After that, her parents asked her cousin to accompany her."

"Did they know who attacked her?"

"No, it was just the once, luckily. And, with her cousin being with her everywhere she went, she was okay."

"What's her cousin's name?"

"Can't remember, sorry. He didn't really sit with us," she recalled, her tone softening. "He would drop her off, and then, when she was ready to leave, he would pick her up. Her parents paid him a salary to drive her everywhere. It was like he didn't have a job or something. I don't know. I only saw him a couple of times, and he was very quiet. He gave me the creeps, but he was her cousin. So …" She shrugged.

"You don't have any pictures of him by any chance?" I

asked, still browsing the various frames on the walls. Perhaps we missed something the first time we glanced at them.

"No, he didn't like having his picture taken. He might have been odd, but Issy never complained about him or anything."

"Thanks, Felicity. We appreciate you speaking with us. One last question, did you know a Mildred Bordeaux?"

"No," Felicity answered quickly.

"If you think of anything, please contact us." James handed her one of his business cards.

Once we were outside and walking toward his car, he handed me one too. "In case you ever need to get hold of me."

"Thanks," I smiled, opened the car door and climbed in. "Is it just me, or did the two girls respond too quickly when asked about Mildred?"

"Yeah, I caught that too."

Chapter Twenty-One

WE STARED at the house for any sign of movement. The storm had long gone, but the grey clouds still surrounded us. It was late afternoon, and the sun we hadn't seen all day was setting.

When a light came on, illuminating the living room, we knew someone was home. If Dr. Eltringham was still as ill as his wife had portrayed, he should be home.

My head throbbed as I pondered this case and all its complexities—Issy, Mildred, Rosemary, Bianca, and the possibility of others. Two of the women had similar appearances as Issy, yet Mildred was one of the first patients who had disappeared, but she looked differently. And James had someone investigating the others. The coincidences involving the doctor and his wife were too great to ignore. And then there was Todd, the boyfriend to two of the women. We needed to determine whether he had a connection to Issy or Mildred.

James sighed beside me, as if we were thinking the same thing.

"Have you ever had such a complicated case before?" I asked, staring at the house.

"I must admit, you sure know how to pick them."

I glanced at him and was greeted with a smirk.

"And, for the record, this one is complicated. It might get worse with our doctor who has already lost a child. But we have to ask him questions about Issy and the others." He climbed out the car and rang the doorbell.

The nurse answered the door. Her blond hair was pulled into her signature tight bun on top of her head. Her dress accentuated her curves. She blinked blue eyes at James. "Yes? Can I help you?"

"Mrs. Eltringham?"

She nodded.

"I'm detective James Michaels. This is Dana Mulder. Would you mind if we came in and asked you a few questions?"

"Why?" The lines between her eyes deepened. She still hadn't acknowledged me, and she gripped the door handle and had closed it somewhat, as if she didn't want us to see inside the house.

"We'd like to ask you questions about your husband's patients and your daughter Issy."

"Why? She's been dead for two years."

"Would you mind if we came inside?" James glanced at me then back at Mrs. Eltringham.

Her eyes flittered from James's then to mine, finally acknowledging me. "Fine. Come in. But I've already spoken with that one" She pointed at me but opened the door for us.

James leered at me.

I shrugged.

He waited for me to enter first then came in behind me.

Mrs. Eltringham walked inside and stopped in the door-jamb between the living room and the kitchen. She folded her arms, waiting impatiently for our questions. "I fail to understand why you need to ask me questions about my daughter's death. It's bad enough she's dead, now you come in here, bringing up the past," she said to James and ignored me completely.

Since she wasn't particularly happy to have me here, which James had noticed, he continued with the questioning. "Again, apologies for our unannounced visit. We're working on a missing woman case."

"Yes, she"—she pointed a long bony finger at me—"was here, and I already told her we don't know that patient."

James ignored her statement and continued sternly with his questions. "Someone took Bianca Edwards from a hospital where it's alleged *your* husband was supposed to have been treating her. It has striking similarities to a case that happened last year, where a Rosemary Haynes disappeared. She too was scheduled for an appointment with Dr. Eltringham. Do any of these names sound familiar?"

She shook her head, and her face glowed with sweat. "No, I don't know these women." She moved farther into the kitchen. "Can I make you some coffee?"

"No, thank you. Are you sure you don't recognize any of these names?" James asked again.

"Sorry, I don't."

"Is your husband home?"

Mrs. Eltringham whipped her head around to stare at us. "No, he is at the medical center."

"I thought he was off sick. That's what the sign said," I retorted.

"He had to check on a few things. And he does have the flu." She said the last part quickly, as if gaining the answers from the air around her. "You can't have a doctor breathing his germs on his patients, now can you?"

"Can you tell us about your daughter's accident"

"It was a hit and run."

"And the attack?"

Her eyes widened as large as saucers, the blue of her eyes darkening. "How did you know about that?"

"We spoke with Felicity and Rashika."

She paled, and her stone-cold demeanor slipped slightly —but not for long. "We don't know who it was, just some boy playing a prank."

"Then why have her cousin act as her bodyguard?"

She flinched as if the words had burned her. Just as she was about to answer, the front door opened.

"Mary?" a male voice yelled. "Whose car is in our driveway?"

A nervousness I hadn't felt in a long time engulfed me when I heard the doctor's emotionless yet enraged voice.

He entered the kitchen, shaking his wet coat. His dark, wet hair lay flattened against his head from the rain. I hadn't heard the rain start again. "Who are you?" he barked at us, throwing a bag onto the kitchen counter, and stood beside his wife, pulling her closer to his body.

"Dr. Eltringham?"

"Yes. Now, who are you? What do you want with my wife?" He squeezed his wife's shoulder possessively, and I actually felt sorry for her.

She cowered under his protection and stared at the floor.

James introduced us again and explained why we were here.

Dr. Eltringham glared at James. He was an imposing figure who made it obvious he didn't want us in his house.

Dr. Eltringham walked out the kitchen toward the foyer and opened the front door. "I'm sure my wife has already answered all your questions. I think it's time for you to leave."

James and I followed, but we didn't exit.

"We'd appreciate it if you could answer our questions as well," James demanded. "Or, if you prefer, we can go to the station for your statement."

"I don't know those patients, and my daughter died years ago. Now please leave."

"I understand you've just returned from your medical center, but would you mind if we took a ride there, so you can show us around?"

"Why?" he asked, angry again.

"You might be the last person to have seen Bianca alive, Dr. Eltringham."

"I've just told you she wasn't a patient of mine." He grunted, veins on the side of his neck popped.

"Here's a picture of her." I held up the photo Ned had given me. "Maybe you'll recognize her."

He skimmed over the picture; I saw hesitation. Dr. Eltringham eyed his wife. "We didn't treat her."

"Dr. Eltringham, we would like you to check Bianca's name in your system."

"You can't ask that," he said, his voice rising in agitation.

"If you do this willingly, we are there maybe ten minutes, and then we're gone. If you resist, I'll need you and Mrs. Eltringham to come down for questioning, and I'll get a search warrant to have fifty of my finest cops ransack your medical center. You're a person of interest in a missing woman case. And we aren't accusing you of anything. We want to look at your center and ask you about Bianca.

Perhaps you just forgot you consulted with her." James approached the front door and stood in front of Dr. Eltringham.

They were the same height, and James had become relentless. He stood his ground and stared down Dr. Eltringham. He might be a doctor, but we knew something was off about him, and we needed to find the evidence to back us up.

"Fine." The doctor grabbed his jacket and headed toward his car. "Come, Mary. Lock up behind you."

We drove behind the Eltringhams until we reached their medical center. I noticed Abe digging in the trash to my right, coming up empty-handed.

He eyed the Eltringhams and waited; I could only assume he was waiting for Mary to bring him food or something.

But she ignored the homeless man, shook her head to warn him off and walked behind Dr. Eltringham who tugged roughly on her arm.

Dr. Eltringham opened his medical center and stood by the door, allowing us entry, then pushed Mary forcefully inside. The reception desk stood before us with chairs lining either side of the waiting area. A narrow hallway was off to one side where patients would walk through to the consultation rooms.

"We are here. Now what?" Dr. Eltringham scowled and stood to one side.

"We found a red top in the trashcan outside that may belong to Bianca. Do you know anything about it?" I asked.

The doctor and his wife shook their heads. "It's a public area. Anyone could've left it there if it was hers," Mrs. Eltringham said.

James walked behind the reception area. "Mrs. Eltringham, do you work reception, or do you help your husband with the patients?"

"I help in both areas, Detective, but mostly with my husband in the consultation rooms," she said quickly, glancing at her husband then back at James.

Dr. Eltringham nodded once. He regarded his wife as if they shared a secret language we weren't privy to.

"Would you mind switching on the PC? I'd like you to check the name Bianca Edwards for me."

Mary did as requested, but nothing came up in the search.

"Who else has access to your records?" James asked.

"Just us and our receptionist."

"We have a credit card receipt from your medical center, which clearly indicates that Bianca was here. How would you explain that?"

"Sometimes patients pop in to purchase medication," Mary explained, stealing a glance at her husband.

"Isn't it a requirement that all patients be recorded, along with the medication prescribed?"

"It is, but somehow this Bianca wasn't. Perhaps she did something illegal."

"We'll be looking into it. In the meantime, I'd like one of our technicians to stop by."

"Not without a court order."

"If you insist." James punched numbers on his phone. Before he could speak, Dr. Eltringham stopped him.

"It's fine. Bring your technician. I don't have anything to hide."

"Thank you. Would you mind showing us around?"

Reluctantly, Dr. Eltringham opened each of the four consulting rooms. He was the only orthopedic surgeon who worked here and was mainly for those on low-cost medical insurance plans. He did not perform any surgeries here, as he did those at the orthopedic center.

An office sat at the end of the hallway, lined wall to wall with files and patient folders. Behind a locked door which he didn't bring the key for was where he kept the medical supplies. He was the only one who had access to it because of the medication stored there. When asked what type of medication he kept, he gave a general answer for painkillers or cortisone he used to inject directly into the inflamed areas.

If Dr. Eltringham was kidnapping women, he wasn't holding them here. It was too risky. The parking lot was out in the open, and anyone could see him coming and going. And, if he was carrying someone, everyone would see him.

Bianca was not here. He had to have another place if it was him—a place where he could freely move the women. I reassessed the facts and that he had property apart from his house—two storages and apartments in California and Florida. Neither apartment would suffice; they were too far. I made a mental note to check the addresses for the storages.

"Do you have any other residencies in the area?"

"No, just our home. Why?"

"Just making sure."

When James was comfortable he had sufficiently checked every room, we thanked the doctor and his wife and advised them we may drop by in the next couple days with more questions and that a technician from the station would contact them today.

Dr. Eltringham agreed, even though I could tell by his expression he was unhappy.

It was then I realized he had no bedside manners and

was surprised he was a busy doctor. I wondered how he was with actual patients.

As we left, I eyed Abe who was waiting for Mary. But she didn't approach him; instead, she climbed into her husband's car with her head lowered, and they drove away.

"Okay," I said as James drove. "He has two storage facilities that I want to check out."

"You realize we can't open them."

"I know, but, if he is keeping women somewhere, I want to make sure we've checked everywhere."

"And don't tell me how you know all this." He shook his head. "But I've asked the uniform to pull his records anyway, so we have a clean trace of how we came about the doctor's various properties."

"Admit it," I said, grinning.

"What?" he asked, concentrating on the road. There was more traffic than usual for a Saturday evening.

"You're having more fun with me than you do with my brother."

James chuckled. "Yeah, just don't tell him that."

Speak of the devil and he will call. My cellphone rang. "Yoh."

"What are you and James up to?" Donnie spoke so loudly James glanced in my direction, shrugging.

I waved him off. "Who wants to know?" I chimed, childishly.

"Dana, don't start. One of the uniforms is CC-ing me on the emails he is sending James. Are you guys working the case?"

"Yes, we're working together. If those two knuckleheads didn't do their job properly last year, we wouldn't be in this situation, Donnie." James winced.

I realized James hadn't told my brother he was helping me. I mouthed, *I'm sorry*, when he glanced at me.

"What happened last year?" He sighed.

I realized I hadn't spoken to Donnie about Rosemary or Mildred yet and cringed.

"Sorry. With everything going on, I forgot to tell you what I'd found. Another woman has been missing since last year. It was a case Stuart and Lip were working on, and they didn't do their due diligence. They didn't connect the dots. Now we have two missing women and one dead one. But we don't think the dead one fits our doctor's MO. She had dark hair. Anyway, I'm rambling. I or James will fill you in with all the details."

James hissed beside me.

"Do you need my help?" he asked hesitantly.

"No, we got this. Spend time with your family. Send my love."

"Call me if you need backup, and bring James over for lunch tomorrow."

I glanced at James, but his concentration was all for the road as the rain belted down on us again. "Uh, okay, sure. Does Mom know?"

"I'll tell her," Donnie said then hung up.

After ending the call, I switched on my laptop to check the addresses for the storage facilities.

Chapter Twenty-Two

THE NIGHT MANAGER of the first storage facility was helpful and even offered to open the doctor's lock for us to have a peek inside. James was about to decline when I elbowed him and shook my head.

"We only want to look. We don't have to go inside."

James narrowed his eyes at me, mouthing, *It's illegal.*

"I know, but it's now or never. We have to know what's inside, otherwise we're doing all this for nothing," I whispered.

The helpful night manager walked ahead of us, wiping his sweaty palms down the side of his stained white shirt. He wore brown pants that hung low and showed off a hairy ass. We reached the doctor's rented storage unit, and the manager opened it for us. The metal doors rolled up, and we stared at the contents.

I blinked a few times before registering exactly what it was I was staring at—a shrine of sorts. A poster of his daughter's face hung on one wall with items she must've had in her room—a folded duvet, mirror, diary, pens, brush, and a baby album.

I took my cellphone from my pocket and snapped pictures.

James frowned at me. "You know we can't use any of this."

"I know, cowboy, but I'm only an investigator, remember? You're the one who needs the law on your side. And besides, nothing here is useful. He comes here to remember his daughter. Nothing is wrong with it. It's just creepy," I said, staring at the items. "We agree this should be at his home and in her old room, like a typical grieving parent, not in a storage facility." I turned to James, who was just as engrossed by the items as I was. "Now I can't wait to see what's in the other one."

———

THE SECOND STORAGE facility was not as interesting as the first. The night manager, Linda, couldn't take her eyes off James though. If I wasn't with him, I was sure she would've ravaged his body and made him cry afterward. He pushed me between the two of them as we followed her to the doctor's storage unit. I giggled when James kept having to move me in front of him.

"This is it," Linda said, eyeing James hungrily for the hundredth time. "Do you want to grab the other side, hun?"

He obliged hesitantly and opened the metal door with her while I stood between them, stifling a laugh.

"This guy is quiet, pays on time and never leaves a mess. Not like the others." Linda eyed the wrappers on the ground near one of the other units. She flicked the light switch and illuminated the boxes on the ground. Against the far wall was a standing mirror, an antique dresser, and a vanity. "I think he moved to a new house or something, if I remember correctly." Linda tapped her index finger on her bottom lip, still ogling James. "He said he only needed it for a few months at the most while they renovated the house."

I widened my eyes at James. We needed to find out whether he had another property somewhere. And, if it wasn't in his name, it could be in his wife's.

We didn't want to riffle through the items in the unit, so Linda and James closed the metal door, and we thanked her for her help. I forgot I had to walk between them, so, when I felt James's hand reach for mine, I realized what I hadn't done, but by then Linda already had an arm through James's and whispered to him. His arms pebbled at her words while I laughed into my hand.

Once we were in the car, I burst out laughing. "Are you all right?" I tenderly rubbed his shoulder closest to me.

James shook his body like he was trying to get rid of the awful memories.

"What did she say to you?"

"Ugh, you don't wanna know." He shuddered again then thumbed through his cellphone. "Let me check to see what the officer sent your brother and me. Maybe she included a list of the doctor's properties." After a moment, James grunted. "Mary has property in her name, and it's in the industrial area."

"Let's go."

————

NO LIGHTS WERE on anywhere in the industrial area. Some buildings had been torn down with only shells left, while others were still in use. The address was for a small building on the far side of the industrial area near a deserted bridge. A chill crept up my spine with flashbacks of Pig-head and all his animal killers hunting us under a bridge similar to the one we had stopped under.

"Are you okay?" James asked, climbing out the car.

"Yeah, let's check it out," I said, following him. The sooner I forgot about Pig-head, the better.

The building was a double story with glass for walls. James tugged on the front doors. They were locked and chained from the inside. "Let's go around," he said, walking in that direction.

We stepped over a low wire fence with one end torn down. Graffiti marked one side of the wall, and, as we rounded the corner, I saw the back door ajar. Both James and I had our hands on our weapons.

"Are you going to call in for back up?"

"Not yet." James switched on his flashlight as he opened the door.

The creaking of the metal echoed down the hallway. I followed him inside, the darkness swallowing us from behind. Nails scratching against floorboards echoed, and the inside was colder than it was outside.

James stopped when we heard the scratching sounds. His frown matched my own under the dim light.

Our feet were quiet against the broken floor tiles, passing room after room. We entered a large area where tables stood at various angles with broken sewing machines atop. When we were certain no one else was inside the first floor, we relaxed somewhat.

"Did the missus have a sweatshop?" I asked, running an index finger over the desk and coming away with a thick layer of dust. Wiping my finger on my pants, I went to the next dark area to see what else we had.

"Nothing was in the files the officer pulled for us. I'm not sure what this place used to be." James walked in the opposite direction toward the far wall.

I flinched when his cellphone chimed.

He glanced at the screen then at me. He answered, speaking softly to the person on the other end.

I couldn't hear what he was saying, but now and then he raised his voice, not sounding happy. I searched the hallway and found a flight of stairs in a dark corner. With only the light from my cellphone to guide my way, I ascended. With my gun pointed ahead of me, I saw the rooms on the first floor were bare, weathered by years of emptiness. Five offices were upstairs, each empty apart from the few pieces of furniture. It was like the occupants had to leave in a hurry for fear of an unseen enemy.

"Anything interesting?" James asked.

My heart stopped beating when I heard his voice, and I pointed my firearm at him.

"Sorry. There's nothing here. It's late. Are you hungry?"

I worried we were running out of time but also cognizant we couldn't work all night long. And, at the moment, we had exhausted all other leads. Until the officer helping James provided more information, we had to sit tight, and I was hungry. "Yeah, sure," I said, holstering my gun. "I could eat now."

Chapter Twenty-Three

EVERY SUNDAY, we ate lunch at my parents' house. It was a formal affair, and everybody had to attend, unless we were dying somewhere; only then would they excuse us.

Upon arriving, my mom ran out the house when she saw James walking up the path. It was like I wasn't even there. She hugged him and pulled him inside without glancing my way. Donnie had arrived the same time as us, and we both shared a look, rolling our eyes.

"You told me to bring him. Look at the effect he has on Mom." We grinned. Donnie wrapped his arm around my shoulders for a sideways hug.

His wife Eleanor held the two younger boys' hands.

I blew kisses at her and the boys. "Hi, Mom!" I yelled at Mom.

She stopped, waved at me and continued talking to James in hushed tones.

Once we were inside, my dad smacked James hard on his back and shook his free hand; Mom held his other hand. They peppered him with questions about work and how he was settling in at the house, blah blah blah. Donnie had brought him for lunch the first month they had partnered up. Since then, he had joined us for lunch at least once or twice a month. And, for my parents, it was like having another son in the house.

Once they finished with James, he looked flustered.

Donnie pulled him aside as they poured themselves a glass of whiskey.

"Hi, Mom," I said again, hugging her. Her floral perfume tickled my nose and reminded me this was where my home was. "Now that you're done chatting to your *sons*, do you think you can spare some time for your daughter?"

"You are my favorite child," she whispered. "Just don't tell your brother." Her grin was contagious, and I smiled and hugged her again.

I sat with her in the kitchen.

Eleanor joined us with a large glass of wine in her hand.

"You okay there, Eleanor?" I asked, jerking my chin at her glass then hugged her.

"Your dad will bring yours now," she answered then had the longest sip I'd ever seen her take. "And yes, everything is fine now." A smile flirted across her face.

"That good, aye?"

"Orgasmic," Eleanor purred.

"Girls!" Mom said, gasping.

We burst into a fit of laughter.

My dad entered, holding two glasses of wine equally as full as Eleanor's. He handed one to me and one to Mom.

"Thanks, Dad," I said, finally getting the chance to hug him.

"How's my Dana-bean?"

"Good," I said and kissed his cheek. "How's the business?"

"Growing. I've hired part-time help." He eyed Eleanor. "To do most of the admin work I can't get around to during the day. Otherwise, I need to work weekends."

"And I said no to that idea. He has worked enough weekends during our marriage that I had to put my foot down. We're lucky to have someone like Eleanor who is available and trustworthy to help your father."

"Does he pay you well?" I asked Eleanor.

"Too much, but I'm not complaining." Her cheeks glowed a healthy shade of pink which I suspected was from the now half-empty glass of wine.

"She looks after those three boys with no complaint. Somebody has to look after her." My dad winked at her.

"That's Donnie's job, Dad," I said dryly.

"Donnie's always at work, and besides, she needs to treat herself. And, with the money I pay her, she can do all those things and more."

"Thanks, Dad." Donnie entered and placed his arm around him. "It gives Eleanor something to do when the boys are at school in the mornings. And it keeps her out of trouble."

Eleanor punched him on the shoulder.

He grabbed and kissed her like he did at their wedding.

"Get a room," Mom yelled as she continued preparing the food.

Leaving the family to banter amongst themselves, I found James alone in the living room. "What are you doing here all on your lonesome?"

"Just enjoying the view," he answered, staring up at me hungrily.

I felt my cheeks flush and blamed the wine. I sat beside him.

"I've been here a few times, and I still don't know what

type of company your dad has." James turned slightly to face me.

"Dad owns a consulting business to help other businesses with their finances. He's an accountant, and it's taken him a really long time to be this successful. Most people his age should be retiring, but he is working harder than ever."

"I see that. Listen … Donnie and I just received word about a body near Grand Calumet River, and it might be connected to our case. We might not stay for lunch."

Before I could answer, Donnie entered and downed his whiskey. "You get the text?"

"Yeah, man. Let's go."

"Mom is dishing up for us. Let's eat quickly then head out."

"Wait. If it's connected to our case, I need to come with."

"No, Dana, this is police business. We'll let you know if it's really connected."

I sulked but understood.

Donnie and James ate quickly while we served ourselves and sat to eat. James left his car for me to use, and my dad would take Eleanor and the boys home later.

As much as I wanted to leave and join Donnie and James, for once, I took my time. I had another glass of wine, ate lunch slowly and even enjoyed dessert. Mom showed me her latest painting, Dad was looking forward to his hunting trip next weekend, and Eleanor told me about how the boys were coping at school. These were all the things I'd missed, because I was always in a hurry to leave and investigate other families, to bring them their closure. I had my own family right here in front of me, and I didn't realize this until I stood to leave. As much as I wanted to stay, it was getting late. For once, I was grateful for our mandatory Sunday family lunches.

On the way to James's house, I reviewed the various parts of information I had relating to the case. One part kept tugging at my conscious—*Todd*. He knew two of the women, and I couldn't help but wonder if he knew any of the others. James had left before sharing with me the detail he had received from the officer regarding the other women, so I couldn't continue interviewing parents. But I could visit Todd again and ask him questions.

I made a U-turn and headed for Todd's house.

———

THE DARK LORD with its Sauron eyes rubbed its furry body against my legs, forcing me to bend down and scratch soft fur behind his ear. Felix purred beneath my hands, which I felt throughout my body.

I knocked on Todd's door, and he shouted he was on his way, while I entertained the cat for a short while.

Todd opened the door with a shocked expression. "You're back?"

"Yes. Would you mind if I asked a few more questions?"

"Sure. Out here?" He gestured to the seats we sat in last time. "Or inside? I just put on a pot of coffee. Come in."

"Coffee would be great, thanks."

"Did you find Bianca?" He opened the door wider, so I could enter.

"Not yet." His house was warm and smelled like coffee. I noted photos near the fireplace, but it was too far for me to see them.

Todd entered the kitchen, grabbed mugs and poured us

coffee. He set the mugs on the kitchen table, pulled out a chair to sit and scanned the kitchen. "Cream or sugar?"

"No thanks," I said, sitting opposite him. "The reason for my visit"—I sipped the coffee, which was good, really good—"is there may have been more victims." I watched his flawless reaction; he didn't flinch.

He stared at me, waiting for more information.

"And I wanted to ask you whether you knew any of them."

"Sure, I'd be happy to help." He sat straighter in the chair. He focused on something behind me and over my shoulder, but it was only the clock.

"Do you have someplace you need to be?"

"Uh, no. I was just checking the time, that's all."

I retrieved my notebook and reviewed the names of the women we thought may have gone missing the last two years. As I flipped through the pages, Todd shifted in his seat again. He seemed agitated about something. I ignored his odd behavior and read outloud the women's names. While I read each name, I glanced up to see his reaction. His stoic expression was hard to read, and I wasn't sure whether he really didn't know any of the women or if he was trying his hardest not to show that he recognized any of their names.

When I finished, I closed my notebook.

He shifted then abruptly stood.

My reaction was to stand with my hand on my gun. "Are you sure everything is fine, Todd? You seem a little distracted."

As he opened his mouth, a noise chimed somewhere inside his house. He pursed his mouth. Beads of sweat peppered his forehead, and he shook his head. "No, I'm fine. Let me get that quickly." He darted through the other doorway that led down a dark hallway.

Not wanting to follow him but still needing him to answer whether he knew any of the women, I went into the living room to wait for him. I needed easy access to the front door in case I had to get out quickly. Todd was up to something, and nobody knew I was here. I needed to defend myself if Todd tried anything. I heard him open a door somewhere, pull something out and slam a door again. Footsteps then silence.

Frowning, I approached the fireplace that had caught my attention when I had first arrived. Photos portraying various stages of Todd's life—some with his parents then later without—sat on the mantel. On the opposite wall were more picture frames. Gasping, I covered my mouth with my hands. A spine-chilling feeling engulfed me. In one picture stood the good doctor and the nurse Mary with Todd's parents. Todd was a young boy, and beside him was Issy, who seemed to be around the same age as Todd. Wiping my hands on my pants, I flinched when he spoke.

"That's my parents and my uncle with his wife." He approached.

"Dr. Eltringham is your uncle?" I asked, still not quite believing it.

He nodded. "My dad's stepbrother." He stalked closer to me with a predatory gaze.

I backpedaled until I hit the wall. My hand squeezed the handle of my weapon.

"Yes, he's a surgeon," he said gravely.

Todd didn't share the same last name and I'd never said Dr. Eltringham's name when I first visited Todd, only referred to a procedure Bianca had been scheduled for. If I'd said something then, I'd have known they were related sooner. Cursing to myself, I now had a bigger problem. What if they were working together? That only meant one thing; I shouldn't have come here alone. A daunting predicament I now found myself in.

Perhaps I could get out of here in one piece by blaming the uncle.

"Todd, do you know your uncle is the orthopedic surgeon who we believe performed procedures on Rosemary and now Bianca?"

Todd blinked at me, perhaps not believing me, and shook his head. "Just because they consulted with him doesn't mean he did anything to them."

"What if you're wrong? He sees you with these girls and decides to take them for himself."

Todd stepped closer and licked his lips. "My uncle would never hurt a fly. He comes across as strong, but he is weak. Your assumption is wrong."

"What if we're right?" My pulse beat loudly in my ears. I had to get out, but I was cornered.

"Prove it." He stepped close enough that I could feel his breath on my face. "You smell good," he whispered hoarsely; his fingers caressed stray hairs near my neck.

He was delusional or in denial, or whatever psychotic state he was in. As much as I wanted to shoot him, I couldn't, not yet anyway. I could return with Marc or James or even Donnie; perhaps they should arrest and question him regarding his involvement. This was a police case, and I needed to hand this over. If it involved Todd and his uncle, they needed to see a prison cell. This wasn't something I should handle on my own. I was stupid to come here alone. Why didn't I just go home?

"I have to go." I cringed when I touched him to pass.

Todd caught my arm, his fingers gripping tightly,

squeezing. "You can't go. I haven't given you the information on the other women's names."

"It's all right. I'll be back. But I really have to leave now." I pulled my arm free, but he had me in a vise grip. "Let go!" I pulled again, but he jerked me closer. I struck him with the butt of my gun, and he released me.

"Bitch!"

I ran for the front door and bolted out of there, running to James's car with his keys in hand for a quick getaway.

Chapter Twenty-Four

DONNIE HAD TOLD me to meet them at the river where we used to fish with our dad when we were kids. As I drove up the road, red and blue lights flashed with a row of police cars and the hearse. They had found a body, and Donnie had suggested I come look; I might be able to identify her.

"Just as long as I don't see the rest of her body, then I'm there."

"You have to. It's part of our case," Donnie had said.

Stones crunched underfoot as I descended the bank to where all the uniforms were hanging around. The yellow tape was up, and uniforms stood guard, ensuring the reporters didn't get through. The same officer who had asked me so many questions at the restaurant leered at me as I approached.

I wanted to growl back at her, but James came up behind me with a hand on my back and led me through.

She scowled silently; her eyes narrowed in my direction. If she could kill me with her dagger eyes, I'd be dead.

"What's up with that woman?" I asked James as we approached the black bag on the ground.

"Who? Officer Jones?"

I nodded.

"Ignore her. She's like that with everyone."

Donnie was speaking with Captain Dodd as we approached. The black bag hadn't been closed all the way, leaving her wet strawberry-blond hair visible.

"Is that Bianca?" I asked no one in particular. I couldn't tear my gaze from her hair; in some parts, it was darker. If I had to guess the cause of death, they had most likely hit her on the head or had left her unconscious in the water, and she had drowned.

"No," James said, moving his hand from my back, leaving a chill in its place.

"No?" I asked.

He nodded.

"How can it be no? Who else could it be then?"

"That's why you're here." He moved us around the others until we reached the top of her head. He knelt and pulled open the black bag, so I could see her face.

I blinked down at the body. Her pale flesh had wrinkled from being submerged in water for quite some time. Her natural wavy and long strawberry-blond hair was stained in her blood. Her crystal-blue eyes shone like lifeless gems, staring up at nothing. A deep gash split her top lip in two. Her open mouth revealed her top two teeth; one had chipped. Someone had hit her hard in the face, most likely rendering her motionless before bludgeoning her head. A bruise on her left cheek had blossomed yellow and green, most likely from a few days ago.

James pulled the bag all the way open, revealing her entire body. She wore a pale blue floral dress; the flowers reminded me of blue lilies best reserved for funerals. Shuddering at the depressing thought and for the woman at my feet, I was relieved my lunch didn't repeat on me. As a PI, I wasn't accustomed to seeing such grizzly murder scenes. This was only the second time Donnie and I had crossed paths because of the cases we shared.

Glancing into honey-brown eyes that held sadness, I nodded at James. "This is Rosemary. She went missing last year." I swallowed hard. Yep, my lunch was about to launch right out of my mouth. Covering my mouth with my hand, I ran toward the trees a few feet away. When I'd finished vomiting, I ignored the sympathetic stares and stopped beside James again.

"You okay?"

"Yeah, think there was something in my mom's food," I said, trying not to cringe.

"We can stand back if you prefer. Not sure whether it's the water or the body that smells like foul fish."

"Perhaps we should stand farther back." I covered my mouth again and squeezed my eyes shut for a moment. Shaking off the dreaded feeling, I stared up the embankment instead. "I have a photo of Rosemary. Her mother gave it to me when I visited her. I can show it to you when we get to your house. I left it in my folder."

"Great." James lead me up the path to where the cars were. "I don't think it's necessary for you to stay here. Perhaps go back to my place, and I'll see you in a short while."

"I need you to come back with me, James. Before Donnie called, I was at Todd's house. He and the doctor are family. The doctor and Todd's father are stepbrothers. I don't know how we missed this, but we did. They could be in on it together, as we suspected. And, while I was there, he tried to grab me—"

James swore, cutting me off, and frantically looked me over. "Did he hurt you?"

"I'm fine, but you guys have to bring him in. And the doctor."

He nodded, searching the area for someone. When he set his sights on the person, I turned to see who he was looking for.

Donnie jerked his chin in our direction, said something to Captain Dodd and headed our way. "Everything okay? Can you tell us who it is, Dana?"

"She was just telling me it's Rosemary. She has a photo of her at my house we can use to confirm before we have her mother make the official positive ID. And we must bring Todd in for questioning. He and the doctor are family, and he dated the deceased and our missing woman. And he attacked Dana."

"What?" Donnie yelled. "Are you okay?"

"Guys, I'm fine. Really. Todd just scared me, that's all. But he needs to be brought in for questioning, the sooner the better. Whoever took Bianca has either realized we're looking into her and they killed Rosemary, or they had to make space for Bianca and got rid of Rosemary." My hands were on my hips as I paced between them, more thinking aloud than speaking to them.

"And you think Todd and the doctor are both involved?"

"Absolutely. They must be. Todd finds them, seduces them, while the good doctor takes over." I bit my thumbnail.

"Stop biting. Mom will skin your hide." Donnie pulled my hand from my mouth.

"It's a habit," I growled at him, and the lines deepened between my eyes.

We were running out of options. We weren't aware of any other places where the doctor could keep these women. The warehouse we had found was empty, except for the medical center. I remembered the walkthrough the doctor did for us and the one door he didn't show us.

"There's a door in his medical center he didn't have the key to. Perhaps he keeps the women in a room there? Alternatively, when you bring in Todd for questioning, check his house. Maybe they keep the women there," I said, remembering the weird noises coming from somewhere in his house. "While I was there, Todd was busy with something in one room. And it sounded odd." I walked toward James's car.

"Where do you think you're going?" Donnie asked, following close behind me.

"I'm going with you."

"No, Dana, you're going home." He opened the car door for me. "If you don't go to James's house, I'll send that female officer home with you." He glanced at Officer Jones.

I scowled at my brother, but he wasn't buying it and paid me no attention. "Fine." I climbed into James's car. "Will someone get the photo of Rosemary?"

"I will when Donnie drops me off later. Don't wait up." James grabbed the door and dropped to my eye level. "Try to get some sleep." He straightened and closed the door.

Starting the car, I opened the window. "Let me know how it goes with Todd."

Once out on the road, something caught my eye. I glanced in the rearview mirror, but all I saw was the empty road behind me. The sun had set, and darkness enveloped the road. I was glad to leave the crime scene behind me, and, even though I wanted to be there when they questioned Todd, I knew I didn't, not really.

Where did Mrs. Eltringham fit in the grand scheme of things? She had to be part of it somehow, or at least knew what her husband and nephew were doing. But what bothered me the most was that she allowed it. Then again, she cowered when the doctor spoke, averted her eyes, answered when spoken to. She didn't want to risk a confrontation when Abe was hanging around the trashcan near their center.

Bright lights refocused my attention to the road. I flicked up the rearview mirror to see the road but kept looking back at the car behind me. James's house was another twenty minutes away. Being naturally suspicious, I didn't want the car to know where I was going. Turning left at the next road, I assumed the car would pass me, but they followed. As I approached a traffic light and it went from green to orange, I hit the accelerator and sped through. The car behind me followed at a much faster speed than I'd hoped. When I came to another turn, I took it and continued above the speed limit. The car was right behind me. Its lights weren't on its brightest, but they were bright enough to cause alarm. With my heart hammering in my chest, I knew I had to lose them.

Up ahead, an old woman driving a much older car sputtered across the road to drive in my direction. She hadn't looked my way as she crossed, but I hit the gas pedal and sped past her. The old woman continued driving slowly and gawked at me; her mouth opened and large eyes stared at me. The car behind me slammed on its brakes, or they would've hit the old car. The old woman realized what had happened and raised her hands, yelling first at me then at the car that had almost hit her. Luckily for me she'd boxed in the car, forcing them to stop, reverse and go around her. But, by then, I was gone.

I performed a little dance of joy in my seat and continued driving like a bat out of hell and did my best, so the car couldn't see where I went. I drove down a dark driveway and parked, killing the headlights. My clothing stuck to my body, and I steadied my breathing. The car cruised by slowly, the occupants bathed in shadows, so I couldn't decipher how many there were. After counting to ten, I pulled out my hiding spot and drove in the opposite direction as the car.

Chapter Twenty-Five

I ARRIVED at James's house with no other headlights in my rearview mirror. The road leading to his mini mansion was quiet, and, since his house was on some kind of timer, all the lights were on by the time I parked in his garage. Once the garage door was closed and I was in the kitchen, I was ravenous now the adrenaline had worn off. I rummaged through his kitchen cabinets for something to snack on. In his fridge, he had an opened bottle of wine and half a roast chicken. I poured myself a glass and picked meat off the small carcass like a vulture.

While I stuffed my face, I opened my laptop and browsed through the information Billie had sent. Unfortunately, there was nothing new. From what I could tell, everything still pointed to the doctor and Todd. And because we didn't know of the family dynamics, Billie didn't widen the search on relatives. If I had asked him to do that, we would've known about Todd long ago. I made a mental note for next time.

I left the photo of Rosemary on the kitchen counter, so James could see it when he got home. He could use that as identification before they contacted the next of kin. I did not want to be part of that team and was happy to remain a little PI who closed cases.

Staring at the picture, I felt Rosemary seemed carefree. Her blue eyes burned with life, a stark contrast to the corpse I had seen earlier. Staring at the roast chicken and the piece of white meat in my hand, I realized I wasn't hungry anymore and threw it away and downed the glass of wine. I placed the rest of the chicken in the fridge and showered.

When I was ready for bed, I placed my Glock on the bedside table and flicked off the light switch. Just as I was getting comfortable and almost asleep, I heard James open the front door, walk quietly across his living room floor and most probably went to his room. I didn't hear him again. I was in two minds whether I should get up and speak with him about Todd or wait till morning.

Knowing my hive-mind, I had to speak with him tonight, otherwise I wouldn't be able to sleep. I needed to know what had happened and if they had arrested him. I climbed out of bed and opened the bedroom door to darkness.

"James?" I called out, entering the living room. The furniture was bathed in shadows. Even the kitchen light was off. James had to be showering. I knocked on his bedroom door.

"Hmm," he replied, opening his door for me to enter. The only light in his room was his bedside lamp.

"James?" I entered and turned to face blue eyes staring back at me. Those were not the honey-colored eyes I was used to seeing. A black mask covered his face with only his bright eyes showing. In my momentarily frozen state, all I thought about was I had left my Glock beside the bed, and I needed to get it. If Pig-head was going to hurt me, it would be a painful and drawn-out process.

In anticipation, Pig-head reached to grab me.

I hit away his arms and ran to the en suite bathroom since he had blocked my exit. I had to get to my room for my gun, or I could lock the door and climb through the window and escape through the trees. When I reached for the key to lock the door, there wasn't one. I swore under my breath, and the door flung open, hitting me on the head. Falling backward, I landed on my ass.

Pig-head stood in the doorway. He was built like a mountain, and there was no way I could fight him; he was taller and stronger.

I pulled open the cabinet, but it was only cleaning materials and nothing I could use against him.

"I'm thrilled to have you all to myself, Dana," he said huskily. He almost sounded out of breath from my attempt at getting away. He stepped closer, his gaze darkening the longer he stared at me.

I didn't want to continue being the object of his evil affection. There had to be something in this bathroom I could use against him. Pushing myself against the cabinet, I decided I would kick at him if he came closer.

He didn't, but he crouched. We were eye level. His penetrating gaze was like a knife on my face. Again.

"What do you want?" I whimpered, scouting the neat bathroom, not seeing anything that could aid me.

"You, Dana. Ever since that night four years ago, all I've ever wanted was you. You enthralled me," he said, rising. His broad shoulders seeming bigger than what they were just a moment ago.

Blood rushed to my head, and all I heard was my heart thumping loudly in my ears. My vision tunneled, and all I could see was his blue eyes. Falling backward, I hit my head against the cabinet. Then I slowly slipped onto the floor. My eyelids were heavy, closing, and a weight was on my chest.

My eyes fluttered open what felt like only a minute later, and Pig-head was straddling me. I was still on the bathroom floor with him on top of me, his mask near my face. He was so close I could smell him—musk and sandalwood. The rest of my senses were useless, and my arms were lead against my sides.

"Women are so predictable, always going for the wine after a long day at the *office*." I could hear him smile behind his mask. "But you're different. You sensed me near, didn't you? You knew I was here and had to come find me." He moved hair out of my face and traced a finger along my jawline, like he was admiring the scar he had made.

My fingers twitched. I could move them, even if it was only one at a time. When I could ball them into a fist, I tried lifting my arm. When I could lift my left arm, I swung it as hard and as fast as I could.

He concentrated on that scar, and, while he was distracted, I hit him in the ear. Pig-head fell to one side off me.

"Get away from me, asshole!" I pushed myself into a seated position, my legs still heavy. I had to get to my Glock while he was down. Leaning on my elbows, I dragged my body. My toes tingled, and I wiggled them, then my legs didn't feel as heavy as they did before. I got onto all fours and crawled.

Pig-head grabbed an ankle before I could pass him.

I kicked as hard as I could. After the fifth try, my heel connected with his face with an audible smack.

He cried out in pain, but, instead of slowing him down, it enraged him.

I crawled faster but not fast enough.

He leaped in the air and fell on top of me, using his dead weight to pin me beneath him, his breath hot near my ear. "I've seen how your detective looks at you, and I don't like it. Tell him I'm coming for him." He licked my face, leaving a burning sensation.

Bright lights flashed against the wall of James's bedroom, followed by a car door slamming.

Pig-head grunted in displeasure and pushed my face hard into the carpet. He climbed off me and disappeared into the darkness of the house.

The front door opened. I bellowed a shrill scream, warning him. Gun shots went off, and the back door slammed shut, followed by silence.

"Dana?" James yelled. The headlights still shone on the wall. Another car door slammed shut, followed by footsteps.

"I'm over here, James," I said, pulling myself off the floor. The ground spun as I stood. I leaned against the wall as James rushed in, finding me, and pulled me into an embrace.

"What happened?" Donnie asked, running into the room. "Are you okay?"

"He's gone. We got here just in time," James said, cupping my face in his hands. "Jesus, your face." James walked me to his bed and sat me down. "I'm getting the first-aid kit."

"I'm calling an ambulance." Donnie left the room with his cellphone pressed to his ear.

I wasn't sure what they were going on about. I didn't remember being hit in the face that hard to warrant their concern or an ambulance. A mirror hung on James's wall. With the last bit of energy, I stood and walked over.

"Don't!" James yelled, running back into his room.

But it was too late. I saw what Pig-head had done. He had left his calling card on my face.

Chapter Twenty-Six

THE PLASTIC SURGEON had stitched me up as best he could, but the fine outline of a pig's head was clearly visible, with bruising that had already started. They tested my blood, and the results showed I had been roofied. Hence, it gave Pig-head enough time to carve the outline of a pig into my cheek. Other tests revealed he hadn't done anything else to me, which I was relieved to hear.

The councilor had just left, offering me the standard advice meant for victims. But I would not fall prey to be his victim again. I would not let someone like him have that power over me. He had already scared me once before, and I didn't like being scared, and I refused to stay scared. And certainly not by someone like *him*.

Dr. Adams had called after I left a message about what had happened. I had a tele-consult for twenty minutes and scheduled an appointment for next week.

Donnie and James entered my private room, their eyes cast downward and their shoulders sagged, suggesting something was up.

"Hey, what's going on with you two?" I sat upright and pulled the covers to my chest.

Donnie sat beside me on the bed. "How are you holding up?"

"I'm fine. Now what's going on with you two? Both of you look like you're at a funeral."

"Nothing." Donnie glanced back at his partner then at me. "We're making sure you're all right."

"Get down to business, guys. I've been out for over a whole day. I've missed a lot. What happened with Todd? And Rosemary? Did you find the picture, James?"

He nodded, panning from me to Donnie.

"Christ, what is going on with you two?"

"The doctor is gone," Donnie blurted. "After we brought Todd in for questioning, we phoned the doctor, but his wife said he went for a drive. He hasn't been home since yesterday. It's been almost two days."

"That's because he's with the latest girl he kidnapped. Did Todd help him?"

"He says he isn't involved and doesn't know anything about it. He's lying of course. But we have someone following him."

"Is anyone following Mary?"

Both men nodded in unison.

"Can you trace the doctor's cell?"

"He left it at home." James spoke for the first time since entering my room. He still looked a little shaken.

"What's up with your partner, Donnie? He looks like he's seen a ghost."

"Will you excuse us?" James asked Donnie, who nodded, kissed my good cheek and left us alone. He closed the door when Donnie exited.

I stared up at James, waiting.

He sat where Donnie had. "I was worried. When I found you looking like that—" He shut his eyes, shaking his head. "If we didn't come home at that time, who knows what that bastard would've done to you."

"It's not your fault, James. Pig-head planned this. He had been following me and waited until I was alone. He drugged the wine. If you were with me and drank that wine, he would've done much worse, because both you and I would've been knocked out."

He nodded, but it didn't look like he accepted this version of my truth.

"Listen, you couldn't have done anything that would have changed what happened. All we can do now is catch the bastard. But first, I need to get out of here." I lifted the covers, winced and swung my legs over the side.

"Wait." He stood. "You can't leave. The doctor hasn't discharged you yet."

"If our doctor is gone, we need to figure out where he went. I've already been out more than a day. We need to catch him."

"Before you dress, I need to tell you something."

I stopped what I was doing and stared at him.

"We found out who the doctor was who operated on Issy, their daughter. It was Dr. Bordeaux."

"The first victim's father, Mildred Bordeaux?"

He nodded.

"I thought she was just a random woman and didn't fit the profile because of her dark hair. But now you're telling me her dad operated on the Eltringham's child. They must've blamed him when Issy died on the OR table." I chose a shirt and pants from my night bag. "How did you find out?"

"It's election time, and having a dead woman and

another one missing on Captain Dodd's watch doesn't sit right with him. He gave us five additional uniforms to assist us with the case. We cross-referenced ours with the list we got from Marc. This morning, we visited the families, including Mrs. Bordeaux. During our investigation, we found Mr. Bordeaux was a doctor and worked with Dr. Eltringham."

I pulled on pants as I considered this information. "It all makes sense. Their daughter dies, the doctor takes his revenge on his friends' daughter. And slowly, he starts unravelling, kidnapping women who resemble his daughter, and then last year, he starts making mistakes with patients. And now, he's disappeared when you want to bring him in?"

James nodded.

"I mean"—I opened the bathroom door and stood behind it while I slipped on my shirt—"it's as if he was preparing for this the moment we started asking around about Bianca."

"Exactly. We're thinking the same thing."

"Remember when we went to one of his storage units, the manager had said he was busy moving or renovating a house?"

"Yes."

"Did you find out whether they have any other properties?"

He shook his head. "No. It could be he told her a story to put his stuff there. We also searched the property in Mary's name, and that too revealed nothing."

"So where are we going?" I came out from behind the bathroom door dressed, sat on a chair and slipped on socks and shoes.

He sighed, knowing I wouldn't just sit by and allow them to have all the fun.

Chapter Twenty-Seven

BIANCA WOKE IN NEW SURROUNDINGS. The walls were a pastel green with painted flowers and leaves. The bed was comfortable, with fresh linen—a cotton and lavender fragrance. She threw off the duvet, sat upright and allowed her legs to dangle over the side. She was a little too short to touch the floor from a seated position. She scooted off the bed and stood in one spot until the dizziness passed. Once the room was no longer fuzzy around the edges, she walked to her new bathroom.

Amazingly, nothing hurt. Her shoulder was feeling better than ever. When she moved the arm that had been operated on, it was devoid of any popping sounds or pain. The pain medication he had given her was most likely still in her system.

This bathroom was bigger and had a shower and a bath. The other room had a smaller, almost medically stifling bathroom, and it only had a bath. She used the toilet and washed her hands. The mirror above the sink hid a cabinet. She pressed on the side by the circle, and the light illuminated, and the door opened. Inside was a new tooth-brush, toothpaste, soap, tweezers, a disposable razor, mouth-wash, and a loofah.

"Good evening," the imposing voice said.

Bianca flinched and spun around, knocking the cabinet door which banged closed. She stepped backward until her ass touched the sink. She placed her hands behind her back and braced herself.

"No need to be afraid." He entered the bathroom but stopped a few steps from her. "Do you like your new room? I made it available especially for you."

She swallowed hard. "Who was here before me?"

"It doesn't matter anymore. It's yours now."

"How long will you keep me here?"

The man in the kabuki mask shrugged. "That will all depend on you, Bianca, and if you behave."

"Please, can you stop drugging me? I will do whatever you need, just stop with the drugs. It makes me nauseated and dizzy."

The man stared at her for a long time, considering her request. She noticed his eyes were a dark blue; that was the only part of him visible from behind the kabuki mask. For a moment, they looked familiar.

"You have one chance, Bianca. I will allow this, but disobey me once, and I'll punish you."

She nodded. "I promise."

"Good. I've brought you some food. You must be hungry."

She nodded again.

"Come." He proffered a gloved hand.

She hesitated at first, remembered his warning and took his hand.

"Good girl." He led her to the desk near the only

window across the room. On the table was a salad and a glass of orange juice. "Sit."

She obeyed.

"Eat."

While she ate, he delicately played with her hair and slowly brushed it, not pulling at all. As he brushed one strand, he held it with the other hand and brought it to his nose to smell, inhaling deeply. Every time he did that, it sent waves of goosebumps all over her body, as if he knew the effect it had on her.

When her bowl and glass was empty, Bianca watched the man in black close the door, then she heard the familiar sound of a lock clicking shut. She shuddered. Realization flooded her—whoever had taken her did so for a reason, and she would be here for a while. As she stood in the middle of the room, beholding her new surroundings, she noted that whoever was here before her was most likely dead. And that she had to—no, she needed to—obey the man in the kabuki mask. She hadn't seen Mary again. And Bianca wondered if Mary was dead too. But she didn't care for long.

Chapter Twenty-Eight

JAMES DROVE, Donnie sat shotgun, and I sat in the back. While I was having my face sewn back together and rested, they had met with all the families who had missing women they suspected were linked to the case. There were nine women in total, including Bianca, Mildred, and Rosemary. Over the years, only three bodies had been found, but the cases were never connected, because the different precincts investigated them. All except Mildred had strawberry-blond hair, were under twenty-five but older than eighteen. Like Bianca's case, they were scheduled for a procedure with Dr. Eltringham and never seen again. And it all started after Issy died two years ago.

James handed me the case file for the investigation into Issy's car accident with photos from the scene. In some of the pictures, there's a crowd of people. I brought the one picture close to my face to study the individuals. In the front was a man who resembled Todd. I gasped.

"Guys, can we get this picture enlarged?" I shoved the picture between the two men.

"I think so," Donnie said.

"I want to know who this is." I pointed to the man. "This looks like Todd, but I want to be sure."

Donnie took the photo from me to study. "Shit!" He checked the back for the serial number, grabbed the radio and called the station. He read the number to whoever had answered. "Nice call there, sis." He glanced over his shoulder. "I see you still got it."

I punched his shoulder. "Of course, I still have it. It never left me."

As we parked outside Todd's house, Donnie's cellphone chimed. He glanced at the message. With both thumbs on the screen, he enlarged the picture. He showed me his cell. The photo was still a little grainy, but it was clearer. And there in the crowd stood Todd with a smirk.

"That tells me he caused the accident," I said. "You guys should look into his parent's car accident as well."

"I'm starting to hate this guy," James said as we reached the front door. He knocked a few times, but nobody answered. "I guess he's not here." He grabbed the door handle and opened it with force. "Oops, that's a very flimsy door."

"I'm going to tell your captain," I teased as we entered the house.

"You aren't even supposed to be with us," Donnie said as he closed the door.

"Your captain gave me permission." I stuck out my tongue at Donnie.

"Todd? Anybody home?" James called, but only the noises from the fridge hummed in reply, and the ticking of the clock on the wall.

"When you arrested him, did you guys search his house?"

"We did, but there was nothing of interest."

"I swear something was in that room"—I pointed to the room on the right—"when I was here. He went in there to do something."

"We can check it again, but it's just a bedroom."

James entered the room first and opened the closets. Hanging inside were old winter coats, boots, and hiking shoes at the bottom. On the shelves were stacks of papers, folders, and a few albums.

I grabbed the album and paged through it. Inside were pictures of Todd and Issy. The first few were random shots in motion and of them individually then with the two of them together. Todd's arm was either around her shoulders or waist, but, in each of them, it was a possessive gesture. Todd was smiling in each of them, his face relaxed and happy. But Issy was unsmiling. If I had to guess, she seemed sad while her eyes screamed for help. If I didn't know any better, she was scared of him. The middle section of the album was empty. I wanted to return it to the shelf, but something told me to look at the back. When I did, I saw more pictures of Todd with other women, all but one with strawberry-blond hair and two I recognized—Rosemary and Bianca. None of them looked happy.

"Guys, look here." I lifted the album for them to see. "I don't recognize any of the others, do you?"

James paged through and nodded. "Yes, they are the missing women."

"Jesus," Donnie said. "Does he date them first for his uncle to take later?"

"We need to bring them in now." James said what we were thinking.

We walked through Todd's house but found nothing else suspicious, so we closed the front door as if no one had just broken in. As we approached their car, their radio sounded. Donnie ran and answered the call. As I opened the back door, Donnie ended the call.

"I can't remember all the codes, but was that a suicide?"

Donnie turned to look at me. "Yeah. It's our doctor." He faced forward in his seat and buckled in.

"He killed himself?"

Chapter Twenty-Nine

THE FLEA BAG motel we stopped at was not a place I would associate the good doctor with. It looked like the place where people paid by the hour. It was a three-story brown building with a green stripe running horizontally on the wall at hip height on each floor. Paint chipped in the corners and peeled away around the dirty windows.

"You need to stay here, sis," Donnie said with a calm hand on my shoulder then leaned in and spoke near my ear. "But we'll give you feedback when we're done."

"Thanks." I stopped near the police tape as the two men crossed the parking lot and entered the room. I stood for a few minutes and tried to catch a glimpse of what was happening inside the room, but I couldn't see much.

The curtains were drawn; it was filled with cops and the coroner. Standing outside the room were a couple of uniforms watching the people who, myself excluded, were most likely renting a room here. A few passersby stopped to look but carried on walking. A woman wearing the bare minimum hunkered out a room, covered her face and ran around the corner. Her *John* exited the room soon after her and disappeared in the opposite direction. Those still standing around lost interest and headed to their respective rooms.

I too was losing interest and walked around the parking lot.

The manager's office was a stand-alone building to the left of the motel. The manager leaned against the wall with an unlit cigarette in his mouth.

"Hi," I said as I neared him.

He turned his beady blue eyes in my direction and gave a curt nod in greeting then continued to watch the police show. "I already told the cops I saw nothing."

"But you do know who died in there?" I thumbed behind me.

He nodded.

"Do you remember how his behavior was when he paid for the room? How many days did he pay for, and did he pay cash? Did he seem a little off to you? Or suspicious?" I leaned beside him against the wall, watching the event before us like a couple of friends bonding.

He snorted with laughter, his attention still on the police. "Do you always ask so many questions at once?"

"Yeah, sorry, bad habit." I shrugged even though he wasn't looking. That too was a habit.

"Did he do that to your face?"

"No." I touched the plaster on my face.

"You a cop?" He turned to give me his attention then, and his brows knitted together. Sunspots littered his olive face, and a faint scar marked the left side of his face from eyebrow to under his ear.

"No, but I'm investigating a missing person case."

"Was he the missing person or the one taking people?"

"The one taking. Young women," I added for effect. If the manager had anyone in his life whom he loved and perhaps if he knew what type of person Dr. Eltringham really was, he could tell me more than what he had told the police.

The manager sussed me out.

I shifted uncomfortably in his gaze and fought not to cover the plaster on my cheek again.

"He was angry when he arrived. Booked a room for two days and paid cash. He seemed a bit confused. I can't say what was wrong, just something seemed off about him."

"Can you think of anything else at all?"

He was quiet for a few seconds then pushed himself away from the wall. "Follow me."

I entered the office behind him and stood near the counter while the manager went into the closed-off back section.

He returned holding something. "I don't know why, but I like you." His gaze flicked to the wound on my face. He opened his hand to reveal a silver necklace. "This dropped out of the man's bag while he was in here paying. My girlfriend likes jewelry, and I wanted to surprise her with it, but, if this helps you find the women, then I'd rather help you."

I took a tissue out my bag and opened it up for him to drop the necklace on. It was thin and delicate looking; one tug and the links might snap. Hanging on the chain was a gem with a white cloudlike streak running through its blue coloring. It was absolutely mesmerizing. My arms pebbled. I recognized it from somewhere. I'd seen it when I paged through the photo album but couldn't remember which woman it belonged to.

"Thank you. Appreciate you helping me." I closed the

necklace with the tissue and pocketed it. "You didn't happen to see where it fell out, did you?"

"He only had one bag with him, and, as he grabbed his wallet, the necklace fell out. The thing is so dainty it didn't even make a sound. I waited for him to notice it, but he didn't. Finders keepers and all, you know?" He shrugged.

"Yeah, I know. Thanks for telling me though. I appreciate it."

"You going to tell them?" He jerked his chin toward the room where all the cops were buzzing around.

"Not yet." I smiled and returned to James's car and leaned on the trunk until they emerged out of the room.

They were speaking with the coroner, and behind them, the body was pushed out on a gurney, nicely wrapped in a body bag.

The hair on the back of my neck stood up, and I turned around, but no one was nearby even though it felt like someone was watching me. Instinctively, my hand went to the plaster on my face. A knot formed in the pit of my stomach, and I stood straight and surveyed the neighborhood behind me consisting of shops, a gas station, and a few houses off to the side. If Pig-head was around, he was hiding somewhere. I didn't know how to describe it, but I knew he was out here somewhere, watching.

I flinched when a hand grabbed my shoulder. I spun around, gripped the hand in mine and pulled sideways.

James moaned as I twisted his hand and elbow, and his shoulder made painful clicking sounds. "Shit, sorry." I released his hand.

"Jesus, Dana, please don't kill my partner," Donnie said as he approached.

"He gave me a fright." I turned around again, still nothing.

"What's wrong?" James asked, cradling the hand I'd twisted against his chest.

"Nothing. I guess I'm still a bit jumpy. Are you okay?" I reached for his hand, but he stepped backward.

"Leave me. I'm fine. We need to write a report." He sounded angry, and I didn't want to push him.

Once we were in the car, Donnie told me what they had discovered. "He was found hanging from the ceiling. But what I found strange was the fingermarks near his neck."

I frowned. "What do you mean? That he changed his mind and didn't want to go through with it?"

"Or …" He glanced at James. "He didn't try to kill himself at all."

Now I was confused. "But you just said—"

"Your brother thinks someone tried to kill him, and I agree with him."

"Why? No one else was in the room."

"One side of his face was bruised, like someone had hit him—possibly knocked him out. Then they strung him up, but then he came to. He clawed at his neck to loosen the noose. He died a slow death."

"Has anyone contacted Mary yet?"

"She's on her way to the station now."

"I don't suppose I can sit in on your conversation with her?"

"No, but you can sit and type our report for us," Donnie half joked. I knew he hated report writing, but it was part of his job.

"I promise to be quiet."

Chapter Thirty

CAPTAIN DODD WAS out for the day, while detectives Wallace and Lip were out on another investigation, so James and Donnie allowed me to sit in the observation room to watch their conversation with Mary. I had strict instructions not to make any sound or they would throw me in a holding cell until they were done.

I also couldn't go anywhere without them due to Pig-head still out there. I sipped on bad coffee and ate vending food—a bag of chips and a chocolate. A day-old sandwich sat in the machine, but I wasn't up for a bout of food poisoning, so I opted for the unhealthy snacks.

James entered the room with a cup of tea for Mary.

Donnie had just told her the circumstances surrounding her husband's death and how they had found him. "Do you know why he was there?"

"I don't know, but—" She wiped away tears and sipped her tea. She exhaled audibly, and her shoulders sagged. She seemed deflated or defeated.

I had witnessed how Dr. Eltringham had spoken to her

and suspected verbal abuse and wondered if her current demeanor was one of relief. Did he physically abuse her as well, and now that he was dead, she would no longer suffer any kind of abuse? With the doctor out of the way, would her life be better?

I flinched when she spoke.

"Nobody knew this, but, when our daughter died, he started forgetting things. I thought it was stress. But then he forgot which patients he saw or what day of the week it was, but he never forgot medicine. He could still operate. When he didn't come home one evening, I went looking for him. I found him disorientated and walking in the streets naked, had bruises on his face like he fell or hit himself. I took him to a neurologist who diagnosed him with the beginning of Alzheimer's."

"Can we have the doctor's details to verify?"

She nodded.

"If he had Alzheimer's, why did he continue practicing?"

"He got confused sometimes, not all the time. He could still practice. That's why he always fought with me. He would do one thing, forget what he was doing and panic. When he was like that, he became angry and would hit himself."

That would explain why his face was bruised or why he had clawed at his neck; he had forgotten what he was doing, then, when he woke up, he panicked.

"Did he ever hit you?"

"No." She shook her head. "Never."

"Did you know about the cases made against your husband?"

"All those cases were dropped, Detective. My husband did not hurt any of those patients."

"What about the missing women?" Donnie listed their names.

She shook her head. "Like I've said many times, we don't have any records for any of these women."

"Do you manage the finances of the medical center you own?" James asked.

"We did together."

"We have credit card receipts for Bianca and others for consultations at your medical center. How do you explain that?"

Mary stammered then closed her mouth. "I've already said that maybe they purchased medication."

"If it was only Bianca, I would understand it as an anomaly, but we have medical claims for three others, Mrs. Eltringham."

"I don't know." She shrugged. "I can only verify what I do know and what our system shows."

"Is it possible someone deleted records from your system?"

"I d-don't know."

"Did you husband ever go out without you?"

"Yes, all the time."

"Were you part of his surgical team at the orthopedic center?"

"No. I helped in the consulting rooms and managed the books with our admin team. He thought it was unethical to have his wife with him in surgery."

"So, you wouldn't know whether your husband kidnapped any of the women from the operating table."

Mary cried and blew her nose. "I can't believe you're talking about my husband like that. It's impossible. He is a kind and caring man. He would never."

"Yet we have evidence telling us he did. And now he's

dead and can't tell us himself what happened. Or where the women are," James said in an accusatory tone.

"That's enough, Detective," Donnie chastised his partner.

She glanced at James in horror, then the tears flowed.

"Mrs. Eltringham, do you know where Todd is?"

She shook her head.

They spoke to her for a few more minutes, but she was too distraught and couldn't answer their questions. They concluded the meeting and asked that she didn't travel, as they might have more questions for her.

She asked where her husband's body was and whether she could see him.

They directed her to the morgue but only after they had contacted her to do so—they were still processing his body.

As they greeted her, I exited the little room and entered the hallway. She would have to pass me to leave the station. I fished the necklace from my pocket and leaned against the wall.

As she walked past, I held up the chain, the little blue gem dangling. Her eyes widened.

"Do you recognize this, Mrs. Eltringham?"

She shook her head. "No, can't say that I do." She strode down the corridor and out the station without looking back.

"What was that all about? And where did you get that?" Donnie pointed at the chain.

"Sorry, brother. The manager gave it to me at the motel. Said our doctor dropped it when he was paying for the room. I wanted to see if the good nurse recognized it, and she did. Now all we need to know is which girl it belonged to." I handed the chain to him still in the tissue. "I doubt you'll find any prints but try anyway."

"I hate it when you do this. But we can't lift prints from a necklace."

"But we can send it to the lab and have them check for any residual DNA from whichever woman wore this," James suggested. "If she had worn this against her skin and not over her clothes, there may just be enough dead skin trapped in the links for the lab to process."

Donnie smirked and pointed an attaboy finger at his partner, took the chain from me and went upstairs for processing.

"I think I remember seeing that necklace in one of the pictures from Todd's album," James said.

"Can you see where Mary is going?"

"That's where I was heading."

I followed James into a restricted area.

He spoke to a guy behind a screen who tapped away on his keyboard. A blimp on a map flared to life on one screen, and it moved away from the station.

Lip noticed I was standing in the room. "What is she doing in here?"

I flinched at Lip's question.

"She's not doing anything, Lip." James whipped around to face the other detective. "But she is helping us on a case you and Wallace fucked up."

"What case?"

"Bianca Edwards."

Lip harrumphed.

"There's more from two years ago, Detective. One you shelved."

"But they're not related." The lines between his caterpillar brows deepened, and he pushed out his full lips in a pout.

"They are. If only you dug a little deeper, her father

wouldn't have hired an investigator to do the job for you. We have at least nine missing women."

"It happens, man. But you're on it now."

"Yeah, we're handling it. You can go back to rescuing cats from trees." James turned to the computer guy. "Let me know where she ends up."

"Sure thing."

"Come, Dana. I'm hungry."

Chapter Thirty-One

JAMES and I were done eating by the time Donnie joined us. He ordered a steak and salad.

"Do you believe her story about her husband?" I asked.

"It's plausible, but we're checking with his doctors to confirm." Donnie bit into his steak and spoke while he chewed. "Mary is at home, and we have a BOLO on Todd. The moment he pops up, we'll grab him."

A thought crossed my mind. While I had been researching Todd, I had found his website and that the printing was done in an industrial area. "Did you search his work premises?"

James nodded. "We did. We met his printing manager who showed us around. It's a small open-plan space with printers, papers, and a small office for the manager. I didn't see anything else."

"When were you there?"

"When you were at the hospital."

"Did you check Mary's warehouse?"

"We checked it all, Dana. We know how to do our jobs," Donnie scolded.

"I didn't mean anything by it, Donnie. I'm just thinking out loud. Perhaps we missed something. And Mary doesn't have any other property in her name?"

"Or maybe the man who did this is dead, and yes, maybe Todd did help out. But until we find him, we must sit tight. Follow the leads, wait for evidence to be processed. I don't want to find another body, believe me, but we've checked everywhere."

I sat back in the booth, emotionally and physically drained.

Donnie pointed at me. "And no, you cannot go snooping anywhere. It's a murder investigation, and I will arrest you if you go near Mary, any of their buildings or look for Todd."

"I didn't do anything." I folded my arms.

"But I know you. I can see your mind thinking of all the stuff you want to do. Stay out of it. I'm warning you. Go home, get some rest. And we"—Donnie pointed at James—"will finish the case."

We left the diner, and James took me home to pack fresh clothing, then we drove to his house. An officer circled his house in case Pig-head returned. He had installed additional door locks for my safety, along with security cameras.

"You know I could've just stayed at my house. You shouldn't have gone out of your way to add all the additional security," I said once we entered his living room.

"I wanted to do it anyway, so it wasn't really for you." James set his keys on the kitchen counter and grabbed a beer out the fridge. "You want, or some wine?"

"No. I'm fine, thanks. Just dropping this off in the

room." I set my bag on the floor in the spare room and returned to the kitchen to see James busy on his phone.

"Sorry, I can't stay." James twisted the cap back onto the beer bottle and placed it in the fridge.

"What is it?"

"Todd."

"I'm coming with you."

"No, Dana." James grabbed his keys and headed for the front door. "You're safer here."

I was not happy to sit at his house while they spoke with Todd. There had to be something I could do. Peering out the living room window, I saw the officer walking around the house and ready to circle again. His partner stood near the driveway. I was stuck no matter what I did.

It was almost five in the afternoon by the time the new shift came. When there was a gap because the cops were talking, I grabbed my bag and exited the back door. I jumped over the fence and entered the forest behind James's house. I could cut through here and find my way to a street and call for a taxi.

As I arrived at the police station, I told the driver to park and wait.

After thirty minutes, Todd exited the station with a man in a grey suit, dark glasses, and a white beard—his lawyer. They spoke for a short while, shook hands and parted ways.

Neither Donnie or James were nearby, and I didn't see anyone tailing him.

"Follow that man," I said to my driver, pointing at Todd.

"Yes, ma'am." He pulled out of our parking spot.

I knew what I was doing was wrong, but we had to find Bianca. I didn't know how much longer she had left or whether she was already dead. And, by the looks of it, the lawyer must have struck some kind of deal to make the police back off.

My cellphone vibrated in my pocket. "Hello?"

"It's James. We had to let Todd go. With the doctor dead and all the evidence pointing to him, we didn't have anything to keep Todd here. And he lawyered-up."

"Is someone going to follow him?"

He sighed. "No. He'd sue us for harassment if we do. Until we have enough evidence connecting him to either the disappearances or murders, we can't go near him."

"What about the necklace? The photo albums?"

"All circumstantial."

"You're joking."

He sighed.

"How much evidence do you need? Him on film and actually killing someone?" The silence stretched between us. I shouldn't have yelled at him; it wasn't his fault—it's the system's. "Sorry, I didn't mean to take it out on you."

"We feel the same way, believe me."

"Okay, when are you coming home?" That sounded so weird coming from my mouth, especially since we weren't dating.

James chuckled. "We're regrouping to find evidence linking Todd or even Mary to the missing women. It might be late."

"Okay. I'll see you later then." I switched off my phone and tucked it into my pocket.

The driver stopped outside a warehouse I'd never seen before and didn't recognize the address. I suspected my driver had pursued someone before, because he parked a block from where Todd had stopped, but we could still see him.

"Have you done this before?" I asked jokingly.

He smiled but didn't answer. That was answer enough.

I watched Todd enter the warehouse, opened the car door and handed the driver cash for the fare.

"Do you want me to stay? This isn't a safe neighbor-hood to be stuck in without a car."

I hadn't noticed the building where we had stopped was rundown with broken windows and graffitied with spray paint. I smelled sewage seeping from the ground. Another building across the street was only a shell of its former self. The only building that still looked great was the one Todd had entered.

I nodded. "Yes, please. I might need to get out of here quickly."

"Yes, ma'am." He cut the engine and turned up Michael Jackson singing "Beat It" from the radio.

I sat again and found the driver's identity card on the dashboard near the radio—*Marty Whittle.*

"Here, Marty." I handed him the card James had given me. "If anything happens to me, call that number and tell him Dana needs help here at this address. If I'm not out in an hour, call anyway."

"No problem." He slouched in his seat, folded his arms and closed his eyes.

"Remember, one hour."

"Yes, ma'am."

Chapter Thirty-Two

THE WAREHOUSE WAS QUIET, but I heard a voice somewhere deep within. I followed the sounds as quietly as I could and was grateful the interior was clean with no debris on the floor to alert him to my presence. When I reached the stairs, his voice echoed in the stairwell. I suspected he was speaking with someone on his cell as I ascended the steps. The railing was clean, as if freshly polished.

When I reached the first floor, I heard Todd's voice above me. On one side of the hallway was a series of empty rooms, on the other side a wall of windows. Peering outside, I could see my taxi driver waiting for me in the shadows. Then at the end of the hallway was a bathroom for women and at the opposite end for men. As I returned to the stairwell, I listened for Todd's whereabouts. The building was quiet.

Tires crunched over gravel, brakes squeaked, and a car door opened. A car was parked beside Todd's. Someone ran down the stairs. I had to find a hiding place before he saw me standing there. I went left and entered the first empty room. The steps continued at a fast pace as he ran down the stairs near me.

As much as I wanted to see who had arrived, I wanted to find Bianca more. Once Todd was gone, I exited my hiding place and took two steps at a time up the steps to the second floor. I traversed the hallway on my left first and found an elevator big enough to fit a small car. Beside the elevator were two rooms with closed doors. Not sure whether anyone was inside the rooms, I pressed my ear against the first door and listened. I heard something …

I flinched when I heard footsteps; someone was coming up. Their voices echoed. Not sure where to go, I turned the knob on the first door. It opened into a medical supply closet.

The steps grew louder as they neared. I closed the closet door behind me with a soft click. Standing in the middle of the room, in darkness, all I heard was my pulse thundering in my ears and my body heating up with a layer of cold sweat on my skin.

The footsteps passed the closet and down the corridor. A lock sounded, then a door opened, and footsteps entered the room beside me. I heard muffled voices and a few words: "eat" "strength" "father" "later". Whoever was in the room next to the closet could be Bianca. Shouting emerged, followed by whimpering. As much as I wanted to go out and help, I couldn't. Not yet.

The shouting continued then a slap. A door opened and slammed shut. The lock turned, and I heard footsteps. My hand froze over the doorknob. The footsteps stopped. I held my breath. Heavy breathing on the other side of the door made my arms pebble. He was there. The doorknob turned, but I had locked it from the inside when I had entered. It stopped turning, and the steps became faint as the person descended the stairs.

Exhaling a shaky breath, I unlocked the door and slowly turned the knob and opened the door. I peered right first then left—nothing.

Standing in front of the other room, I turned the knob. It was locked. With one ear against the door, I heard someone walking around—manic pacing.

I rapped my knuckles on the door then whispered, "Hello? Anyone there?"

"Hello? Who's out there?"

"My name is Dana. What's your name?"

"Bianca—" she choked.

I sighed with relief. "Bianca, your father hired me to find you. Can you open the door?"

"No," she whimpered, twisting the doorknob rigorously, trying to open it. The knob made a noise that I had to grab to stop the rattling.

"Shh! I'll find a way to get you out. But you have to be quiet."

"No, wait. Please don't leave me. What if he comes back?"

"I promise I'll return and get you out. But you must act as if I'm not here, in case he does come back. Do you understand, Bianca? Act as if nothing is wrong."

"Okay," she whispered. "Please don't forget me here. I can't stay here another second."

"I'll be back. I promise."

I pulled my cellphone out of my pocket and sent Donnie a message along with my location. He called, but I let it go to voicemail. Then I sent him another message. *Can't talk, come quickly. Found Bianca. Phone on silent.*

We're coming.

I pocketed the phone and headed toward the staircase. It was quiet. Peering over the banister, I couldn't see any shadows or movement, but I could still hear them.

Unsure whether other girls were here or if it was only Bianca, I had to look. I walked down the hallway and tried the first door on my right. It opened to a makeshift theatre. The room smelled of disinfectant with a copper undertone. In the middle of the room were ceiling-mounted surgical lights, an operating table with straps, sterilization and cleaning equipment, monitors, and screens and wash basins against the far wall. Lining the other side of the wall was a medicine cabinet filled with surgical instruments and vials.

Voices echoed in the stairwell. I gently closed the door and stood behind it in the dark corner. The voices neared and passed. I was about to exit when the door swung open. I stood flat against the wall, hiding behind the door.

"What is it?" a lady asked, sounding like Mary.

Covering my mouth with both hands to quiet my breathing, I was grateful the door was solid, and they couldn't see me.

Silence. My pulse hammered in my ears.

"It's nothing," Todd said eventually and exited the room.

"Did you check on Bianca?" Mary asked as they left.

"Yes, she's fine. But we should get ready to move. With the cops asking questions, they're bound to find this place. We have to find another spot soon."

Sirens wailed in the distance.

"Fuck!" Todd yelled, then they ran. "No, Mary. Leave the bitch. Let's just get out of here."

"She's seen our faces."

"Let's go!"

They descended the stairs.

I slowly maneuvered around the door. I wanted to get to Bianca before Todd returned. I ran out and straight into Todd standing like a block of solid cement near the stairs. My uninjured cheek hit his shoulder.

His arm gripped around my shoulders, and, with the other hand, he pulled my right arm up and behind my back.

My shoulder cracked from the sudden movement, and I winced. A thought ran through my head; was this how he hurt the women? To cause an injury so bad they had to see an orthopedic surgeon. From what I remembered, both Bianca and Rosemary had injured their shoulders and didn't remember how it had happened.

"It's your floral perfume, Dana. You're the only one I know who wears it."

I cursed myself for my stupidity. I should've known.

"Why, Todd?"

"Why?" he repeated, spittle splashing my face. "It's all because they took my Issy away."

"She was your cousin?" I said with disgust.

"No, it's not what you think. I was adopted. Mommy and Daddy found me abandoned at the hospital where Dr. Eltringham worked and took me in. But I was *never* one of *them*."

"They loved you, Todd. Why did you hate them so much?"

"Because they tried to tear Issy from me. But Issy loved me. Then I had to arrange for a little accident for them."

"You killed your parents?"

"Adoptive."

I remembered the album and the look on Issy's face with Todd's arm draped around her, and she was not happy to be there. But I didn't want to anger him and refute his claim. I did want to understand how the doctor was involved.

"Was Dr. Eltringham ever involved?"

Todd squeezed my arm and lifted it higher. My shoulder clicked, sending another violent shudder through my body. When I whimpered, he eased down my arm. My left arm was free and felt for my pocket. I could unlock my phone and launch the voice recording app in my sleep, I used it so often.

"God, no! I already told you he wouldn't hurt a fly. But you wouldn't listen to me. Did you? That poor man was distraught when his daughter died. When I found out it was his friend, Dr. Bordeaux, who had killed her, I knew the only way to get back at him was to take his daughter from him."

"It was a tragedy, Todd. Things happen. You didn't have to kill Mildred."

"I did, and I felt better afterward. But, when my uncle found out about Mildred's death and that I had something to do with it, we fought. He blamed me for everything and said I had ruined their lives and that I should never have been born at all. With Mary's help, I snuck into his medicine cabinet and gave him a dose of his own medicine. He unraveled from the concoction. Bit by bit, he started to forget. He used to go to that shrine in his storage facility, but, after a while, he forgot he even had it." He snorted with a sarcastic laugh. "Mary helped with everything, you know. She pushed me to take Mildred. Then she pushed me to take Rosemary. And all the others, of course, she wanted me to have them. I think it's because Mary liked to watch. Could you guess that about her?"

I shook my head.

"She's very kinky."

I was relieved he was spewing his thoughts as waves of confessions came out, which we would use against him. I didn't want to interrupt him, so I kept quiet.

"Oh yeah, she loved watching me with the women. She fed them the drugs then would open the door wide enough so she could see me. But I didn't like mature blondes. I liked them young, docile, and strawberry. Like strawberries and cream."

I clenched my jaw to stop myself from yelling at him. I needed him to confess to it all.

"The women really did have their operations, here though, obviously. We confused Dr. Eltringham and told him this was the orthopedic center. Mary helped by being my nurse. She also didn't mind that I loved Issy. She was happy for us. She wanted Issy and me to be together as much as I did. Then, when she died, I had to find a replacement."

"Did Dr. Eltringham really kill himself?"

He chuckled sinisterly. "No way he could've done that. The man knew what to do with his scalpel, it was everything else he couldn't do. But I had to get rid of him, use him as a scapegoat. Did it work?"

I didn't answer.

Sirens wailed in the distance

"Shit! Come, you're my ticket out of here." He forced me to walk with him down the stairs.

I was still stuck to his chest and had to step backward down the stairs. I was Todd's shield against the policemen downstairs.

Shouting erupted below, yelling for Mary to get on the floor.

As we reached the bottom, a wave of uniforms

surrounded us, making Todd tighten his grip on me. "Get back, or I'll kill her!"

I felt something cold and hard pressed against my head. Out the corner of my eye, I saw at least a dozen men, all weapons drawn and pointing at us. I squeezed my eyes shut.

"Let her go, Todd!" Donnie shouted.

I smiled; he was the best backup anyone could have. I just hoped his aim was still true.

"I'm getting out of here."

"Either in a body bag or quietly. Now let her go," Donnie said gruffly and moved closer. "Nobody wants to get hurt, Todd. Put down the gun and come with us. We can discuss it like civilized people." Donnie was close enough to grab me.

Heavy-booted footsteps ascended the stairs. Police were behind us. He had nowhere to go.

Todd relaxed his grip on me and sighed. He realized he had to either surrender or die, as he could never get out of such a tight spot.

"There's nowhere for you to go, Todd. Mary is in custody, and the first one who sings gets the deal." I knew all that was bullshit; there was never a *deal*. "Let Dana go and give me your weapon."

As Todd released me, two men on either side came in behind Todd and grabbed him. They pinned him to the ground, disarmed and handcuffed him.

I nursed my shoulder and stepped away.

"Where are you going, Dana?"

"Bianca is in one of the locked rooms. I promised I would get her out."

"I'm coming with."

Chapter Thirty-Three

TODD AND MARY were charged with a shopping list of crimes. The lawyer Todd had used previously excused himself, and now Todd was seeking another defense attorney. Mary crawled into her shell and wasn't speaking to anyone. The recording I had made of Todd's spontaneous utterances could be used against him, and it would assist us in convicting Mary too.

I sat in my office chair, relaying everything to Marc. I had a 4 p.m. appointment with Ned and Bianca. She had been hospitalized for a day; her shoulder was fine, and the drugs they had injected were out of her system.

Because I was adamant something was amiss in Todd's second bedroom, Donnie and James took a sledgehammer to the walls, which revealed a small room with a bed and chains hanging from the walls. A camera was hooked up in the corner. They followed the cord to a device behind tiles in the guest bathroom. The footage on the device was enough to convict and sentence Todd to life in prison—they were pushing for the death penalty.

In the closet with the photo album, they discovered boxes of jewelry similar to the one the motel manager had found. Todd had given each woman one as a token of his *love*. I shivered thinking about it.

It had been a week, and I was still staying at James's house and incident free. Pig-head hadn't shown his swine face again, but we didn't want to take any chances and always had someone with me wherever I went.

Tonight, James and I were trying a French restaurant, and this time, I wore an evening dress.

Chapter Thirty-Four

THE FOLLOWING Saturday morning brought rain and miserable weather. I woke in James's arms. He held me tightly, as if he were afraid I would disappear. A smile crept along my face as he planted butterfly kisses on my shoulder and gently moved up my neck.

"Morning," he said between kisses.

"Morning yourself." I turned around, so I could wrap my arms around him. "How did we end up in bed together?" I teased.

"You kissed me, remember?"

I shook my head. "Nope. I don't remember it happening that way. I distinctly recall you leaning over me with your lips close to mine."

He chuckled and kissed my nose. "Do you regret my advances?" he asked, pushed me back, so he could see my whole face.

Laughing, I shook my head. "None whatsoever. I do need some coffee though."

"Stay here. I'll make it." James climbed out, pulled on underwear and went to the kitchen.

I did leave his bed due to the obvious morning toilet routine. I pulled on my own underwear, went to the bathroom and returned in time for him to bring me my coffee.

He gave me that award-winning smile, handed me a mug and leaned forward for another kiss. "You were saying …"

I frowned up at him. "What?"

"Are you giving me the day?" He pleaded with those honey-colored puppy-dog eyes. He was so hard to resist, and heat crept up my face.

After my last case, I took Marc's advice about a two-week vacation. James took a couple of days, so we could spend more time together.

I grinned. "Yes, James Michaels, I will give you the day, weekend, and even a week for good behavior."

We finished our coffee and readied ourselves. James wanted us to go hiking then enjoy a scenic lunch nearby. The last time I went hiking, I was still in school. He packed snacks and bottles of water into two backpacks. We arrived at the Starved Rock State Park and started our thirteen-mile hike. Other hikers shared the trail, but they kept to themselves. Before we had left, I'd sent Marc and Donnie a message, letting them know where we were. Donnie responded with a childish, *Oooh*, while Marc replied fatherly, *Good girl*.

We stopped at each canyon we were permitted and marveled at the waterfalls. We were both fit and managed to keep a steady pace and passed other hikers along the way. We would stop every couple of miles for a water break and snack on peanuts or a protein bar before continuing.

James told me about his childhood—how they used to move every so often, because his dad was in the military. That's why he had chosen to join and served two tours before settling down and working his way to detective.

We held hands on our hike and kissed. It felt strange being in a relationship after years of being single. For once, I had something other than work to focus on, and I felt great. Somehow James and I were perfect, and, as optimistic as I was, I hoped the other shoe wasn't about to drop. But, before any of that happened, I would enjoy every moment with him.

When we reached the ten-mile mark, we stopped and found a log under a tree for our last break. I finished my water and placed it in my backpack.

"You ready?" James asked, standing a few steps from me. He stretched his hamstrings and walked toward the path.

"Yeah, all good, just need to slip this back on." As I threw on the backpack, movement caught my eye. The figure darted behind a tree. I narrowed my eyes. Out the corner of my eye, I saw James step closer to me.

"What is it?" He knew I had seen something.

"Not sure, but I think someone is out there."

"Come." He grabbed my hand and pulled me to the path. He pointed at rocks and motioned for us to go that way.

We hid behind the rock and waited. James lifted his index finger to his lips, while I nodded. We listened. Someone approached our hiding spot. James pulled me closer to his body. We unholstered our guns. James pushed me behind him and inside a hole in the rock then moved to the front.

The person who I'd seen cowered slowly, searching.

At first, I thought I might have been mistaken, but the way he was walking low, trying to hide his body, suggested otherwise. Our instincts were on par, and now we needed to subdue him and ask why he was following us.

James ran and jumped on top of the guy, surprising him.

He tried to block James, but James was quicker and experienced.

He managed to pin the guy to the ground, with his arms behind his back. Gunshots sounded, hitting James's backpack, sending him to the ground.

I moved around the rocks, my gun pointing in the direction the shots had come from. Another shot. I aimed and fired.

James moaned.

The guy kicked James to the ground and ran.

Taking aim, I shot the guy in his thigh, and he hit the ground hard, swearing.

I noticed blood pooling beneath James. My blood ran cold. This couldn't be happening. Not yet, I'd just met him. We had only just begun to get to know one another. I couldn't lose him now. My mind raced with unwanted thoughts.

I slowly came out my hiding spot. Another shot rang, and I fired, hitting something. I saw the other assailant crying and dragging his leg behind him up the path. I didn't want to leave James on his own, and I didn't want the guy getting away. I grabbed James's handcuffs and ran to the assailant.

He tried to hit me, but I punched him in the face, knocking his head backward. He hit the ground, unconscious.

I pulled his arm and handcuffed him to the twelve-mile

signpost. I dashed to James and pulled off my backpack. I felt for the first-aid kit. Once it was out, I lifted his shirt to assess the damage. Luckily, the bullet had gone through his shoulder. I didn't know whether it had hit any important arteries, but I needed to stop the bleeding. I ripped gauze from the first-aid kit and pressed on the wound.

James moaned in agony.

"Does this feel okay?" I asked once I'd bandaged him and he'd stopped bleeding.

"Just swell," he said, his mouth curving upward. "Here." He handed me his cell. "Call dispatch. We need a helicopter out here."

I did as he asked. We only had to wait ten minutes.

"You must wait for your brother to get here and fetch that one." He pointed at the man lying face down in the sand.

"I want to come with you."

"I'll be all right. You can see me when you're done."

I didn't like the idea, but he was right. If I went with him, the man might escape, and I'll never know why he had attacked us.

"Hang in there, James," I said with his head in my lap. My hands were warm against his head as I brushed his hair with my fingers. Color had drained from his face and his lips had paled. I kissed them anyway.

"Besides this little accident, how was your day?" he asked, making light of a serious situation.

"One of my best days yet," I said through misty eyes. Hearing the blades overhead, my heart hammered in my chest. "Hang in there."

James nodded.

"I'll be there when you wake up." I kissed his forehead.

The helicopter landed, and two paramedics jumped out

and ran to us. They inserted a drip, assessed his wounds and stabilized him in the shortest time I'd ever seen before moving him to the board.

When he was on the helicopter, I kissed him one last time and waited for Donnie to come with backup.

Chapter Thirty-Five

WE WALKED toward the area where I thought I had hit the second gunman. We found shell casings and disturbed greenery behind a tree. Something was lying a distance away from us.

Donnie grabbed it and showed it to me. It was Pig-head's mask.

vinci-books.com/devilmountain

Dana makes a grisly discovery while assisting the police search for a mom and her two daughters on Devil Mountain.

Turn the page for a free preview…

Devil Mountain: Chapter One

LIFTING my camera to my face, I watched my target walk into Tiffany's; my finger eased down on the button and took the shot. A few minutes later, he exited with a pretty pink bag in hand. I snapped another picture. I set my camera on the seat beside me, but, before I could dial my client's number, my phone rang with a familiar name on the screen.

"Hello, Dr. Adams," I said.

"Let me guess. You've forgotten about our appointment today."

I cringed in my car seat; to be honest, I had forgotten. I was so busy following my client's ex-husband to Madison, I'd forgotten all about my appointment with my therapist. "Yes," I whispered sheepishly as I watched the ex cross the road and climb into his car.

Dr. Adams sighed so loud I could hear it as if he was sitting beside me; he wasn't happy. "Okay, I can fit you in at the end of the week. Does that sound good?" he asked carefully. He was very accommodating; I'd forgotten my appointment once before, and he had squeezed me in.

Previously, I'd asked to move sessions, and he always made a plan for me. I supposed once he knew what I'd been through, he really wanted to help me in any way he could.

"Friday?"

"Yep, say four o'clock?"

As much as I didn't feel like it, I knew I had to go. Dr. Adams was a great listener and made me feel comfortable enough that I would open up and tell him what was on my mind. It didn't hurt he was pleasant to look at—dark hair styled right, bright green eyes, and wore glasses when he took notes. He was professional and put me at ease whenever I felt like I was about to spiral out of control. The previous session, I'd left in tears; it wasn't anything he'd said but what I was going through. The nightmares of Pig-head were still haunting me, and every time I spoke with Johnny, it seemed to bring everything to the surface—again.

"Yeah, four o'clock is fine."

"Is everything okay?"

"All good. Thanks for calling. I have to go, see you Friday." I killed the call before he could respond and quickly dialed my client's number before Dr. Adams could phone back.

"Please tell me you have something!" Maddy cried into my ear, the stress of everything evident in her tone.

I stifled a joyous laugh, trying to put myself into a good mood after my call with Dr. Adams but failed miserably, and Maddy shrieked. "I got him, Maddy," I finally said, not wanting to keep her anxious.

Maddy shrieked again.

Her ex had been telling the judge he was bankrupt and unable to pay my client child support. She suspected he had hidden money during the divorce, and he had a new girl-friend by the time the proceedings started, which made her more suspicious. Now with him going into the jewelry story, I suspected the new girlfriend was about to be his new fiancée.

"What did you get?"

"Uhm, he was walking out of a jewelry store." I winced as I said the words. I knew Maddy still loved her ex and was in denial after the divorce. If she knew he wanted to marry another—if what I assumed was correct—I wasn't sure how she would handle it: confront and attack him or continue with the legal route. "Are you sure you want the details?"

"He's going to marry her, isn't he?" She sighed audibly.

"I don't know—"

"Okay, it's okay. It's really okay. Send it to my lawyer and tell him to let me know what the judge says."

I exhaled. That was the best thing she could do for her family. "No problem, Maddy. You just take care of your beautiful girls. Let your lawyer handle the rest."

"I know you're right. And, Dana …?"

"Yeah?"

"Thanks for helping me."

"It's a pleasure."

"You doing this for me, and for free, has helped us. When the jackass starts paying, I will take you out for a lunch somewhere."

"That's perfect. You take care now."

As I ended the call, it rang again. It was Johnny—my direct report when I had worked as an analyst for the FBI. We had kept in touch all these years and spoke at least once a month to catch up. I would even ask him for guidance on cases I was working, and he always obliged to help. It was strange he was calling again, since we had already spoken last week. For him to call again, had to be urgent.

"Hey—"

"Dana! I need your help."

"What's wrong?"

"It's not me. It's my sister."

Grab your copy…
vinci-books.com/devilmountain

Acknowledgments

Thank you to my dearest best friend, Angelique. You have been my ultimate fan, and I'm lucky to have you on my side.

Also, to my family: without you, I may not have gotten this far.

And to my editor. He has been awesome, to say the least. I'm sure he laughs at my South African slang, but he always gives me the right American terminology, and I'm grateful for his input.

Lastly, to my readers, thank you for reading!

About the Author

N. Gray is a USA Today Bestselling Author who lives in Cape Town, South Africa, with her daughter and adopted cat named Miss Beans. During the day, she's an analyst and provider profiler for a medical insurance company. At night, she types on her curved keyboard, creating fictional characters some may love and others you may want to kill yourself.

She writes in four genres: urban fantasy, thriller, horror, and paranormal romance.

She now writes under Natalie Michaels for her new thrillers and SD Syns for her new horrors.